Praise for

Prescott Woods

Bubbles and Troubles is an enjoyable tale. I loved Carmen. She makes no bones about what she wants and finds a way to make it happen. Brock, as Carmen says, needs to grow up! Bubbles and Troubles throws together lots of lore and makes it work in a madcap tale to save Prescott Woods.

~ Erzabets Enchantments

Instant lust between the two slowly starts to spin to love which is soon interrupted by mayhem. Dora's hesitation and conflicted feelings about the changes being asked of her, and the desire for Lowell are present, and fortunately all works for the best interest of the two. *~ Jeep Diva*

Totally Bound Publishing books by Bebe Balocca:

Carved into Her Heart
A Ghost on Two Wheels
Learning to Soar
The Curse of the Tiger
Bent Out of Shape

PRESCOTT WOODS
Volume One

Bubbles and Troubles

Beds and Blazes

BEBE BALOCCA

Prescott Woods Volume One
ISBN # 978-1-78184-671-1
©Copyright Bebe Balocca 2013
Cover Art by Posh Gosh ©Copyright 2013
Interior text design by Claire Siemaszkiewicz
Totally Bound Publishing

Published in 2013 by Totally Bound Publishing, Newland House, The Point, Weaver Road, Lincoln, LN6 3QN, United Kingdom.

Totally Bound Publishing is an imprint of Total-E-Ntwined Limited.

BUBBLES AND TROUBLES

Dedication

To James and to memories of a back road in Georgia

Chapter One

He was tall, lean, and corded with muscle. He slipped through the shadows like mist. Carmen chased him, frustrated, and called out. He'd disappeared into the rustling leaves, and she felt utterly bereft. Would she never feel his touch again?

She whimpered in the silence of the woods, lonely and cold. He was gone, and she was alone.

Then he was at her back once more, solid and warm, towering over her. Carmen leaned into him, overwhelmed with relief and longing.

"You're back," she breathed. "You came back for me. I hoped so much that you would."

He cupped her breast with his right hand and slid his other down her belly. The skin of her abdomen warmed and moulded to the shape of his fingers and palm.

His erection pressed into the small of her back and he moved his left hand lower, yanking down her skirt and panties. Carmen's breaths quickened. She reached behind her and drew him closer, gripping the clenched cheeks of his bare ass with her hand. "Yes," she whispered.

He stroked between her legs, teasing the edges of her pussy lips with the lightest of touches, before sliding his fingers inside. Carmen arched against him and felt wetness flow from her cunt over his knuckles. She writhed in his embrace, twisting her spine so that his hardened shaft ground against her lower back. He shoved his fingers deep within her, stretching her, and Carmen spread her thighs wide. She covered the hand that fucked her with her own, urging him to push deeper and faster.

Abruptly, he forced her to her knees on the woodland floor. Carmen caught herself with her hands and gasped to feel the tip of his cock nudging the entrance to her pussy. She lowered her weight onto her elbows and thrust her ass high into the air.

He entered her with one aggressive stroke. His shaft, impossibly thick and long, seemed too big for her, but her dripping wetness eased the snug entry. "Fuck, yes," Carmen whispered. She feared that she might split into pieces, skewered by that magnificent organ of his. It was a delicious, searing, perfect pain.

She flattened her chest on the ground, bending in two. The dry leaves rustled beneath her, delicate and feathery on her sensitive nipples, as his thrusts shook her entire body.

"Come inside me," she murmured. "Fill me up."

He trembled and stopped briefly, pulling out with elaborate slowness, and gripped her waist tightly. Eager wetness coated Carmen's lower lips.

Then he shoved it all in, fucking her furiously, and came with a roar. She fell into her own shuddering, raging climax. The walls of her pussy contracted in rhythmic spasms, matching beat-for-beat the spurts of thick fluid that gushed from his shaft.

Carmen bucked against him, drawing out her orgasm, and scraped her tits on the leaf-strewn forest floor.

* * * *

Cock-a-doodle-doooo!

Carmen exhaled and pulled her slickened fingers from between her legs. Cool grey light flooded the room.

Once more, that huge stray cat was sitting outside her window on the ledge, staring in.

"Like what you see, kitty-cat?" Carmen asked.

The fluffy grey cat meowed, brilliant blue eyes flashing, and leapt away. Carmen made a mental note to buy some cat food at the store and try to convince the big tom to stick around. Recently, she'd noticed signs of mice in the chicken coop—she could use a good mouser.

Life on Carmen's little farm meant rising at the crack of dawn, but she loved every day of her life in the eastern Kentucky country. She stretched with a satisfied groan and then used a tissue to wipe off her sticky fingers.

* * * *

"Come on, girls! Breakfast time!" Carmen opened the door to the henhouse and scattered scratch feed over the ground. Agatha, the dove-grey Silkie, and Bella, the black-and-white speckled Andalusian, trotted over and began pecking away. Scarlett and Melanie, the fluffy, fancy Faverolles, stuck close together and approached cautiously. The other birds sometimes bullied them. Carmen thought they must be jealous since Scarlett and Melanie were by far the prettiest chickens in the flock.

Gretel, the robust black Jersey Giant, sidled up next to Carmen. Gretel was as friendly as she was hefty. Suellen, the orange New Hampshire Red, worked her way in between Agatha and Bella. Spare Tire, the Bantam rooster, hopped down from his favourite black rubber perch and strutted around his girls. Carmen's mellow golden Labrador, Dax, exited his doghouse and sat by Carmen's feet with a proprietary air. He and Spare Tire had an uneasy truce. Both felt it was their job to protect the girls — the chickens and Carmen — and Carmen had made it clear that peace between her boys was the only option. Dax locked eyes with Spare Tire and huffed, then trotted back to his doghouse to observe the scene from the comfort of his cedar chip bed.

Rewind it all five years and Carmen would never have imagined that she'd be living here in this old cabin next to the woods, with six chickens, a rooster, and a big yellow dog as her foster children. Not to mention working at an organic vegetable co-op. Oh, and belly dancing. *I'm a regular hippie*, she chuckled to herself. City-boy Ian would be totally appalled.

How things change, Carmen thought, scattering another handful of grain for the flock of chickens. Five short years ago she'd been on the career fast track in Chicago. She and Ian had both been corporate lawyers living in Lincoln Park. Ian was handsome, glamorous and driven, so being his girlfriend had been an ego-enhancing thrill ride. Carmen had loved going out on Ian's arm and knowing that all eyes had been on the lean, elegant, fashionable man beside her. Their weekdays — and often weekends, too — had been busy and challenging with legal work, but free time had been nothing but sweet. Fabulous restaurants, the best wine, erudite friends, and trendy parties — Carmen had known she had it made. When Ian had taken her to Fishbone Alley on their three-year anniversary, Carmen had hardly been able to contain her excitement. She had just known he had been going to propose, and it was just like Ian to pop the question in their favourite restaurant.

That night, Ian had shown her just how little she knew. "God, I never saw it coming," Carmen muttered, watching Agatha and Bella take a break from pecking the ground to sip from their water dish.

Ian had waited until after dessert before dropping his bomb.

"I'm glad we had a last special evening together, Carmen, because I wanted us to share a final night together."

Those calm, cool words of his had sucked the blood right out of her face. "Final?" she'd asked, baffled.

"I'd like you to meet someone," Ian had said. He'd beckoned over her shoulder. Carmen had turned and had seen the head chef of Fishbone Alley walking to their table. Chef Morgan Greenway had worked his way across the crowded dining room, smiling broadly at Ian and greeting customers, then had given Carmen a brief nod.

The stocky chef with the face of a seasoned boxer had marched right up to Ian and Carmen's table then he'd taken Ian's hand in his.

Carmen's head had spun. "Are you kidding me, Ian? After three years of being a couple, you're telling me that you're into men? Seriously?" She'd scrunched her nose, trying to make sense of what had been before her. "You're into chefs?"

Ian had cleared his throat. "Look, Carmen, I know it's not fair to you. It's just something I discovered about myself. Well, with Morgan's help." He'd locked eyes with the chef. The two men couldn't have looked more different—Ian, with his delicate, aristocratic features, and Morgan, who looked fresh from a brawl in the alley—but they'd clearly shared a bond.

Carmen's reaction had surprised everyone, including herself. She had laughed.

Ian and Morgan had exchanged confused looks. Carmen had stood up and had tossed her napkin down onto the table.

"I should have seen it coming," she'd managed to force out between loud guffaws. "You're just a little too pretty, Ian, and a little too fashionable for a straight dude. The funny thing is that I thought you were going to propose tonight." Tears of laughter had squeezed out from Carmen's eyes and she'd gripped her shaking sides. An embarrassed hush had fallen over the restaurant. "I'm going to leave you the cheque though, or maybe you can ask your boyfriend to take care of it." Carmen had collected her purse and jacket. "You boys have fun with whatever you do next, okay?"

Carmen had walked past a couple of stunned tables before wheeling back around to Ian. "Give me three days in our house," she'd announced, "to clear out my stuff. Don't come home at all, and don't call me. I don't want to see or hear from you ever again. I want the house sold immediately and I want half of the profits sent to me through my parents. You've got their phone number, right? From those Christmases we spent with them?" Carmen, seething, had swept her gaze around the packed restaurant. Expensively dressed people had filled each table, and every single shocked eye had been on her. The cruel hilarity of the situation had overwhelmed her. "I'm grateful, Ian" — she'd laughed bitterly — "because I see now that I don't belong with you, and I don't belong among these people, and I don't belong in this city." Carmen had marched to the front door with her head held high, had walked out, and had never looked back.

She was snapped out of her reverie by a soft, insistent nudge. Gretel, determined to get at a cricket between Carmen's feet, had wedged her chunky black bulk between her ankles. Carmen tossed the last of her grain to the chickens and replaced the cup in the feed barrel. She eased down into her padded swing and stared into the Prescott woods.

In the five years she'd lived there, Carmen had only made a few short forays into the woods. Somehow, she felt out of place there, even intimidated. She'd attributed it to the fact that she was, in fact, trespassing, and decided to listen to her instincts. Those woods were better left alone. Besides, there was plenty of nature to explore in and around Charade, and plenty of wildlife, both human and animal. Gretel, appetite satisfied at last, clucked and looked up at her with curious black eyes.

She lifted the chunky black chicken to her lap and stroked her glossy feathers. The June morning was already balmy, and soon temperatures would climb into the mid-eighties. The shadowy woods would be dark and cool, though…

Carmen shook her head and gently placed Gretel on the ground. Those woods were off-limits, both because they belonged to Calvin Prescott and because of the creepy vibe they gave her.

She picked up her basket and entered the chicken coop to collect the eggs. Oddly, the chickens had had another light day of laying. Normally, the girls would give her at least four or five eggs every day, and frequently more. Often, Gretel was good for two or three all by herself. The last week or so, however, Carmen had only found two eggs in the coop every morning. She checked the latch on the coop's door. It was secure and hadn't been gnawed by an animal.

Besides, if animals had been getting into the coop, they'd have bothered the birds. And Dax, of course, wouldn't tolerate anyone messing with his chickens. She looked back at the little flock. They all looked robust and relaxed as they explored the fenced backyard. She scanned the edge of the woods for any sign of the huge grey tomcat. "Here, kitty, kitty, kitty," she called out, but there was no sign of the furry grey feline. Apparently he'd gone off to wherever he went when not peeking through her window. Carmen shrugged and went inside to get dressed for the day.

* * * *

Carmen was Charade's only lawyer. However, since the population was so tiny, she only practised law for two days per week. A few real estate transactions, some estate planning, and a more-or-less amicable divorce now and then helped shore up her savings account. On her lawless days — a term gleefully coined by her friend Dora — Carmen worked two five-hour shifts at the local vegetable co-op, Bushel and a Peck. Her other lawless activity involved dancing barefoot to exotic music. Carmen had expected to hate the belly-dancing class that Dora had dragged her to, but instead she loved every minute of the gyrating, sensual experience. After a year of attending classes religiously, she'd become a certified instructor.

Slipping into her black yoga pants and cropped spaghetti strap top, Carmen wondered what Ian would have to say if he could see her now. She was about as far from their Chicago law firm as a girl could get. Carmen placed her hip scarf in her shoulder bag and locked up the house. Even though Dora and Colby had made fun of her for locking her doors in a community like Charade, it was one big-city habit that Carmen couldn't seem to break.

Chapter Two

A quick ride on her Vespa brought her to the rec centre and her small but devoted class. Dora and Colby were on the front row, as usual, along with Bernice, the town librarian. Beth, Hippie Chic's owner and stylist extraordinaire, and her teenage daughter, Monica, made up the back row.

"Hi, guys. Happy Friday!" Carmen said in greeting while tying the coin sash around her waist. "Where's Deb? Is she okay?" She kicked off her shoes and placed them against the wall.

"Here I am!" Deb burst through the door. "And oh my gosh, you all! Have I got news or what!" Deb's curly carrot-red hair trembled with nervous energy. "Marcus and I were at Tie-Dyed and Gone to Heaven, unloading a new shipment of incense and essential oils, and we overheard some folks from out of town. They referred to themselves as the Morgan Group, and they were having a very, very interesting conversation." Deb arched her pencilled brows.

"Out with it, Deb." Bernice rolled her eyes.

"Well," Deb continued, "Marcus and I heard them say that the new development planned by the Morgan Group for the Prescott Woods was going to be the most luxurious and modern one outside of Lexington. Homes are going to sell in the low to mid millions, and, get this…" Deb paused for effect. "They're going to put a nine-foot-tall brick wall around the entire Prescott Woods. Can you even imagine what a thing like that would cost?"

"I don't believe it," Colby stated. She shook her head and her platinum blonde hair rippled down her back. "Calvin Prescott would never sell his family's land for development! It's been in the Prescott family for six generations."

Deb huffed. "I'm just telling you what I heard, Colby. Besides, that man has no children. Who's he going to leave all that land to?"

"I certainly hope it's not true," Dora clucked. "That would mean huge changes for Charade. I don't want a bunch of rich city people moving in. I like our little town just the way it is." She took a sad breath and her ample bosom heaved.

"Ladies, it's time for class," Carmen interrupted. "We're not going to learn anything about this in the next hour, but we can get a great class in. Are you ready?"

Carmen turned on the stereo and led the class through a series of hip drops, shimmies, and kicks. As always, the Middle Eastern music soothed her, but worries bubbled beneath her surface. Were her beautiful woods — well, Calvin Prescott's beautiful woods — going to be cut off from her view by a tall brick wall? Would a passel of the very people she'd left behind in Chicago move into her transplanted hometown? Would they overrun mellow, stuck-in-the-sixties Charade with fancy gourmet food stores and interior design shops? Would the sweet, simple life she enjoyed be uprooted by a lucrative real estate deal?

Not if she had anything to say about it, Carmen decided. She concentrated on her moves, stepping and bending to the music. As usual, she felt a lusciously erotic stirring while she danced. Her bared physique wasn't fashion-model skinny, but belly dancing emphasised the tactile desirability of authentic, healthy curves and exposed skin. At first, Carmen had been embarrassed to feel aroused while she danced, but now she welcomed the sexual energy that sparked through her while dancing. Feeling a sweet, hot slickness grow between her lower lips, Carmen knew that she'd have to finish herself off with some personal attention as soon as she got home. Her nipples stiffened in anticipation. Belly dancing made her feel sexy, nimble and desirable, never mind that she was a single thirty-something woman who raised chickens.

While gyrating her hips to the seductive soundtrack, Carmen glanced up at the window. That same grey tomcat was sitting on the windowsill outside, staring in as though it saw a roomful of flightless birds. It licked its chops. Carmen rolled her eyes and looked away with a smile. *Maybe I'll get my new mouser after all,* she thought, amused, *or, at the very least, a devoted belly-dancing fan.*

The class wrapped up, but her six students remained in the room. Monica giggled with excitement and Beth hushed her. "What's going on?" Carmen asked.

Bernice pulled a gold-wrapped box from her tote bag. "This is for you, dear," she said, handing it to Carmen. "We all chipped in. Happy birthday!"

Carmen took the box and blushed with pleasure. She had completely forgotten that today was her birthday. And it wasn't just any birthday — it was her fortieth. "Thank you all so much," she whispered, choked by gratitude.

"Well, open it!" Monica urged. She bounced on her toes and squealed.

Carmen slipped the ribbon off and opened the box. Inside was a gorgeous confection of bronze silk chiffon and beads.

"It's Turkish!" Monica exclaimed. "Isn't it fabulous?"

Carmen lifted the beaded bikini top from the box and shook it. Long strands of golden coins and beads shook like drops of metallic water from the bronze sequined bra top. "It's so beautiful, guys." Carmen smiled. She passed the top to Dora and held up the matching beaded belt and skirt. "I can't wait to wear it when we perform together for the Fourth of July. This is too much, really. You are so generous, every one of you."

Beth, Monica, Deb and Bernice hugged Carmen then gathered their things.

"I'll let you know if we hear anything about the Prescott place," Deb promised as they departed.

Dora and Colby hung back after the others left. "Let us take you out tonight, Carmen," Dora offered. "We'll drink some beer and throw some darts at the Mine Shaft. What do you say? A girl doesn't turn forty every day, you know." Dora covered her voluptuous figure with a fringed floral shawl.

"We'll pick you up at nine, okay?" Colby confirmed. "It'll be fun, Carmen. I've arranged a cab from Aldridge, so we don't have to worry about driving." She gave Carmen a knowing wink.

"Suh-weet!" Dora crowed with excitement. Her heavy breasts jiggled with merriment. "We'll catch a buzz, okay, Carmen? See you at nine!"

* * * *

That evening Carmen had a simple meal of a grilled cheese sandwich and tomato soup. She took her dinner outside to eat with the chickens. They pecked in front of the dense, mysterious backdrop of Prescott Woods. Carmen chewed thoughtfully as she watched ruddy Suellen chase fluffy, multi-hued Scarlett and Melanie around the yard. *Surely Calvin Prescott wouldn't sell off the woods,* Carmen thought, *when it's been so important to his family and to Charade.*

That huge old stone mansion built by Calvin's great-great-great-grandfather was the most historically and architecturally impressive structure in eastern Kentucky, if rumours could be believed. Calvin Prescott, a noted recluse, refused to allow visitors to his home. The limestone mansion stood half a mile from the road and was veiled by trees, but glimpses of it were impressive nonetheless. A tall wrought iron gate surrounded the mansion and lawn, and the two-hundred-acre forest stretched beyond it.

Carmen finished her meal and gathered her chickens into their coop. They roosted promptly at sundown, so it was best to have them all tucked in before it grew dark. Spare Tire helped her round up the girls then strutted in behind them. She gave the latch an extra tug to make sure it was firmly fastened before going inside to get dressed for her birthday outing. She chose a snug pair of her favourite jeans, a black silk tank top, her dressiest pair of cowboy boots and a chunky handmade agate necklace.

* * * *

At eleven, Dora was bringing around the third pitcher of draught beer at the Mine Shaft. Colby had declared herself Dart Queen Extraordinaire and was loudly challenging everyone in the bar to a match. Vonda Richardson, Charade's real estate agent, was quick to rise to the challenge. Carmen giggled to see dainty Colby—her ear smudged with brick-red paint from her current artistic project—talking smack about her skill at darts.

"Hey, girls!" Deb appeared by their table, radiant in a turquoise tie-dyed tunic and frayed denim miniskirt. "Mind if I join you for a minute or two? Marcus just put quarters on the pool table, so we're up next. Are you having a fun fortieth, Carmen?"

"Indeed I am." Carmen beamed. She hopped from her stool and gave Deb an enormous hug. "Thank you so much for my present, Deb!" she gushed. "And thank you so much for being in my class. I love belly dancing with you guys!" Carmen bounced with beer-fuelled enthusiasm, causing her enormous gold hoops to flop against her neck.

"You are just so welcome," replied Deb. "We love having you in Charade. I bet there's no other small town in Eastern Kentucky that can say they've got a lawyer, belly-dancing teacher, and veggie co-op owner-slash-employee all in one cute little package."

Carmen gave a self-deprecating shrug and rolled her eyes upward. "As far as I'm concerned, there's no place in the world as wonderful as Charade."

Dora poured a glass of beer for Deb from the pitcher and pulled the seat out for her. "So, did you hear anything else about the Prescott land thing?"

"Oh, God, don't get me started," Deb groaned. She downed half of her glass in two big gulps. "It looks like it's going down, girls. Marcus said that while I was at belly-dancing class, a guy in a suit came in and asked where Calvin Prescott lived. Marcus gave him directions, and told him that historically, Mr Prescott did not appreciate visitors." She cleared her throat and tossed back the rest of her beer. "Suit tells him that he's sure Mr Prescott will welcome his visit, since he's about to purchase a great deal of his land and make Mr Prescott a very, very wealthy man."

"Puh-leeze!" Carmen interjected. "He's already a very rich man! Good grief." She poured another glass of beer for Deb and topped off her own glass.

Deb twisted her mouth to the side. "Who knows, Carmen," she said. "Nobody goes up there, and nobody knows what old Calvin's financial situation is. He certainly doesn't bank around here, that's for sure. Marcus's friend Tom is the manager of First Trust in Aldridge, where 'most everybody around here does their banking, and he's already asked about the Prescott money. Tom said that there's no Prescott money at First Trust, so who knows how much Calvin's got squirrelled away."

"Huh," Dora mused. "Maybe he's house poor after all, living in that big old mansion. There's got to be a lot of upkeep to that thing."

"Well, he still doesn't have any right to change the whole flavour of Charade, damn it," Carmen complained.

Deb lifted her hands in resignation. "Well, it is his land after all, so I guess we have to like it or lump it." She waved over Carmen's shoulder and stood with her half-full glass. "Thanks for the beer, girls, and happy birthday, Carmen. I wouldn't worry too much about the Prescott land if I were you. Charade's been around for a long time, and it's not going anywhere."

* * * *

Two pitchers later, Dora and Colby were singing an off-key but enthusiastic version of Happy Birthday to Carmen in a black-and-white Aldridge City Cab. The driver pulled in front of Carmen's house and waited for the ladies to hug their goodnights and for Carmen to exit. While Carmen fumbled for her keys, she heard Dora and Colby resume their singing as the cab eased down her driveway.

Chapter Three

Arr-uff! Arr-uff-uff-uff!

Dax's bark drew her attention to the backyard. It wasn't like him to bark for no reason. Could it be that her egg poacher had returned to swipe another basket?

Carmen clomped in booted feet around the side porch. "Get 'im, Dax!" she shouted as she raced to the backyard. "Get that thing and hold it down, boy!" Carmen rushed through the fence gate towards the sound of Dax's barking, which was, sure enough, right next to the door of the chicken coop.

Carmen saw a tall form in the shadows. Unmistakably masculine and incredibly imposing. Even under the influence of alcohol, she felt the icy tongue of fear lap down her spine. She and Dax were no match for a grown man, let alone a trespasser with bad intentions...

Carmen took a step back towards her house. "Just take the eggs," she said in a shaky voice. "I'm going inside now. Take all you want, okay?" She felt dizzy with dread as adrenaline coursed through her limbs.

With her hand on the doorknob, she stared at Dax, who was barking nonstop, and the shadowy figure. Before her eyes, the figure shrank and moved. Carmen shook her head in confusion. It was...a cat? The big grey tomcat hissed at Dax and darted up to Carmen's feet. *Stupid beer. Thank goodness birthdays only come once a year*, Carmen thought, and opened the back door.

"Here, kitty, kitty, kitty," she called. Noisily purring, the cat walked into her house as if he owned the place, his tail held high. Dax followed, visibly annoyed with the whole proceedings. "It's okay, Dax," Carmen soothed. "We need a mouser around here, boy." She took a rawhide bone from the kitchen cabinet and held it up for Dax. With a sceptical glance towards the cat, Dax chomped the bone and trotted out to his doghouse.

Carmen turned to her new house guest. The huge furball sat on the kitchen floor, staring at her. "So, you're a stray, huh?" Carmen asked him. "You look pretty well-fed for a homeless cat. Have you been eating my eggs, mister?" The glossy grey cat bumped his head against her calf affectionately.

"So, I haven't been to the store yet, kitty, and I don't know what I've got around here that you might want to eat." The cat brushed once more against her leg before trotting out of the kitchen towards Carmen's bedroom.

Carmen followed him and chuckled to see him leap onto her bed and stretch out on his back like a sleeping lion. "Please make yourself at home, kitty-cat." She laughed. Carmen slipped out of her boots and tank top, and yanked her jeans down to her feet. Clad in a silky turquoise cami and hot pink satin boyshorts, she held a hand out to the cat.

"Don't get offended, bub," she slurred, "but I'm not letting anyone into my bed who has fleas. Just gonna do a quick check, okay?" The cat purred like an outboard motor as Carmen parted his thick charcoal fur with her fingers. She shook her head in bemusement at the fearless stray cat baring his belly to her. After a few minutes of careful searching, Carmen didn't find a single flea or tick. In fact, the cat's thick, shiny coat was scrupulously clean and as soft as a chinchilla's.

"All righty then," Carmen decided. "You've got the all-clear to share my bed, mister. Hope you appreciate the honour. You're the only male who's been here since I moved in five years ago." She took a quick bathroom break, washed her face, brushed her teeth, then climbed into bed.

It seemed that as soon as her eyes closed, her dream was back, clearer than ever.

Once more, she was in the depths of the woods. He was inside her, pummelling her cunt with that fat cock of his. He had his hands in her hair, around her waist, caressing her breasts, and she pumped her rear against him in approval.

In a sudden motion, he yanked his shaft from her and whipped her onto her back. Carmen cried out in surprise then moaned in delight. He buried his head between her thighs and parted her folds with his tongue. Carmen lowered her hands to his head. His hair was silky, lush and thick between her fingers. "Fuck, yes," she whispered. He lapped her clit delicately, and Carmen's nipples puckered in response. His hair was so exquisitely soft, it felt almost like fur as it grazed the sensitive skin of her inner thighs. Carmen ran her palms over it, loving the cool, silky feel of his locks and the clever, wet attention from his mouth.

His hands moved to her thighs and yanked them farther apart. The dry leaves and twigs under her ass crunched. Her muscles protested the deep split stretch, but she relished the burn. Oh, God, he was touching her again. He slid strong, thick fingers over the crumpled, wet lips of her pussy as Carmen whimpered, impatient for more. His fingertips found the opening to her cunt and slowly, slowly, slowly eased inside.

With his tongue skidding over her swollen clitoris, he unhurriedly fucked her with first one, then two long digits. Carmen arched and bucked against his hand and mouth, urging him to go faster and deeper and harder, but he seemed to be in no rush whatsoever.

She fisted her hands in his hair in desperation and pulled his face tighter to her crotch. "Do it," she begged roughly. "Make me come again." Carmen cried out when he wedged a third finger between her legs. Her pussy wept at the tight fit. She ground against his hand mindlessly, her body twisting and undulating of its own accord.

She realised with a smile what her dream lover's hair reminded her of. So luxuriantly soft and thick, and unbelievably silky…

Carmen's eyes flew open in alarm. The room was dark, but enough moonglow filtered through the window that she could see her own spread knees on the bed. She reached tentatively between them, her heart thumping, and felt that unmistakable soft fur.

"Oh my God!" she squeaked. "Kitty! No! Bad kitty!" Carmen grabbed fistfuls of fur and yanked the randy thing up from between her legs.

"Ow!" a deep male voice protested. "What the fuck! Ow! Let go, Carmen!"

"Holy shit!" Carmen grabbed the sheet and scooted back against the headboard of her bed. She fumbled for the bedside lamp with one shaking hand. *Click.* Yellow lamplight warmed the room and exposed the naked man tangled in sheets at the foot of her bed.

He had a tousled mane of slate-coloured hair that stood wildly on end, like that of a manga character in a comic book. The man rubbed his head, wincing, and looked up at her with accusing sapphire-blue eyes. "You didn't have to pull my hair out," he muttered. "It's attached to my head, you know."

Carmen gaped. He was the most beautiful man she'd ever laid eyes on. His skin was the colour of buttery, molten caramel. His chest was chiselled and sharply defined, his shoulders were gloriously wide and his biceps were bulky and knotted. And oh, those abs. Carmen let her eyes wander lower. A thick erection, ringed by slate-grey curls of hair, jutted from his lap.

She shook her head. "Am I drunk-dreaming or crazy? Who the fuck are you?" She leant forwards and lifted one trembling hand to his head. That rich, grey hair felt just like the fur of a chinchilla. Or a cat. "Are you the fucking stray cat?" she gasped. "What's going on?"

"I'm not a cat, but, ah, I might have looked like a cat a time or two to your eyes." He seemed oblivious to the still-thick cock pointing towards his chin, but it was incredibly difficult for Carmen to feel the same. She found her treacherous eyes wanting to drift downward, again and again, to drink that luscious sight in. Clearly, it had been way too long since she'd been with a man. Five years, in fact, and Ian almost didn't count, since his heart obviously hadn't been completely into their lovemaking by the end of the relationship.

"And that makes about zero sense," Carmen grumbled. She rose from the bed and yanked her chenille robe around her. Knotting the sash, she glared at him. "You better do some talking, mister," she warned, "or, I swear, I'll call the police right now."

Carmen turned on her cell phone, dialled 9-1-1, and held the phone up threateningly.

"Ah, yes." The man stood and lifted his hands in an 'I'm innocent' gesture. Carmen swallowed with effort. He was at least six foot three and looked uncannily like David Beckham in his skivvies. Minus the skivvies. "I'm Brock. This will probably be a novel concept for you, but, along with members of my family, I have the ability to cast glamours on humans. To change what they see and trick them into seeing something else. I wanted to get closer to you, but I didn't think you'd just let me waltz in, so I made it so that you saw a sweet little cat instead."

"Bullshit," Carmen said. She pointed one finger at the 'call' button and lifted her eyebrows.

"Seriously," Brock insisted. "I'm always truly in this form, but, to your eyes, I was a puffy grey furball." He grinned and added, "You can't really blame me. Would you have let a man peek in your window for your daybreak solo playtimes, Carmen?"

Carmen shrieked in embarrassed fury. She pressed 'call' and tossed the phone on her bed then shoved Brock into her walk-in closet. He fell back on his bare ass with a thump. Carmen saw shock register on his face before she slammed the closet door. She pulled her heavy dresser in front of the door and picked up the phone from her bed.

"I'm here," she told the concerned dispatcher, "and there's a peeping-tom trespasser trapped in my closet."

Chapter Four

Carmen had pulled on some jeans and a sweatshirt by the time the policeman arrived. She waited, tapping her foot, as the young officer exited his patrol car and approached her front steps.

"Good evening, ma'am." Officer Paul Treble tipped his hat gravely. "What seems to be the trouble?" He stood at polite attention on Carmen's porch.

Carmen groaned inwardly. She'd known Paul ever since she'd moved to Charade. As a pimple-faced teen, he'd helped out at Bushel and a Peck during high school, bagging bunches of kale and rhubarb for customers, before going to college and to the police academy.

"Come on in, Paul," she answered. "I caught a trespasser in my bedroom and I've got him trapped in my closet."

Paul placed his hand on the grip of his pistol. "Is he armed, Ma'am?"

"Sheesh, Paul, just call me Carmen, okay?" Carmen insisted. "And, uh, he's not armed. He's not even dressed," she added, blushing.

Paul gave Carmen a sideways glance. She coloured slightly and led him to her bedroom. The tall oak set of drawers stood in front of her closet door, massive and unmoving. Paul put his shoulder to the dresser and pushed it out of the way. He hopped back in front of the door and slid his gun from the holster. Pointing it up to the ceiling, he shouted in a commanding voice, "I'm going to open the door now. Put your hands on your head. Do not move. Do not take a step. Do you understand me?"

Carmen took a step back. Brock might be hot, but he was also a trespasser. And the whole cat-thing was just too weird to even consider. It was just creepy, no matter how you cut it. And who knew what a creepy trespasser might do…?

"Yowwwwrrrr?" a plaintive meow questioned from the closet.

"You locked him in there with your cat?" Paul muttered in surprise.

"I don't have a damn cat!" Carmen retorted. "There's been a stray around the place, though. It must have gotten in my closet."

Paul placed one hand on the closet doorknob.

Carmen had an increasingly bad feeling about the whole situation.

Paul nodded to her and threw open the closet door. He lowered his pistol to chest level, but no one was inside the tiny space. However, a huge, fluffy, grey tomcat emerged, purring heartily. It walked—strutted—into the centre of the room. The cat blinked its bright blue eyes at Carmen. To Carmen, its noisy purrs sounded exactly like laughter.

Damn that Brock.

"It seems that no one is here, Miss Graham. Do you think the intruder could have left the closet and replaced the dresser in front of the door?"

Carmen scowled at the heavy grey cat that scrubbed his face against her shin. "No, Paul, I stayed in my room and watched the door until I heard your car drive up. I'd have heard the dresser move around if he'd gotten out."

Paul raised his eyebrows. "May I ask what time you came home tonight, Miss Graham?"

"Please, Paul, call me Carmen!" she said in exasperation. She glared at the stocky cat by her feet. "I don't know, I got home about one, I think. Maybe it was closer to two, now that I think about it."

Paul nodded. "Out with the girls at the Mine Shaft?" he asked. "Shooting some darts and drinking some beer?"

Carmen felt blood rush to her face. The cat leaned against her leg like a sympathetic conspirator. "Yes, fine, I had some beer to drink. And we took an Aldridge cab home, in case you were wondering. And *no*, I wasn't just imagining an intruder in my house because I had maybe a tiny little buzz from the beer. I saw him, Paul! He was in my bed, touching me!"

Now it was Paul's turn to blush. He turned a fantastic shade of crimson and stared at a spot on the floor. He tipped his hat and turned, not meeting Carmen's eyes. "With your permission, I'd like to check around your property, Miss Graham, to be sure that your intruder isn't, ah, lurking around. You might want to bring your dog in. I'm sure he'd make you feel safer."

"Yes, yes," Carmen agreed. She gave the cat a hate-filled glare and let Dax in. He gave the cat a thorough sniff then settled to sleep on the rug in Carmen's bedroom.

Carmen brewed a pot of herbal tea as Paul investigated. He returned to inform her that he'd seen no signs of forced entry or damage to property. "You might want to hang on to that cat, you know," he added as Carmen walked him to the front door. "Looks like he'd be a great mouser, and you sure could use one around here."

Carmen, fuming, sipped her tea and had a stare-off with the cat until the police car pulled out of her driveway.

As soon as the sounds of Paul's patrol car were gone, Brock appeared in place of the cat in all his bare-naked glory. He was laughing, damn him.

"Can I have some tea, too?" he asked. "That smells great. And do you have a robe for me? It's just a bit chilly."

Carmen rolled her eyes and fetched her robe from her bedroom. Dax groaned in his sleep and rolled over. "Some watchdog you are," Carmen muttered.

Brock tied the pastel robe around his waist and grinned. His corded forearms stuck out from the cuffs and his bronzed thighs and bulging calves were exposed below the hem. The robe was nothing more than a fuzzy mini dress on him, but at least it covered that deliciously muscled chest, sculpted ass, and heavy cock of his.

He ran his hands through his wildly luxuriant ashen hair. "What about an early breakfast? I'm famished. Maybe some of those fantastic eggs of yours, Carmen?"

Exasperated, Carmen poured a cup of mint tea and handed it to him. "Can I have a little more information, please? Like, am I delusional? Or are you the crazy one? Or are we *both* nuts?"

Brock opened the refrigerator door and rummaged through the shelves. Try as she might, Carmen couldn't keep her eyes off his taut thighs, bare and muscular, and the scanty hem of her bathrobe. "Got any cheese in here?" he asked as he bent and searched. The edge of the robe slipped up higher, over the rounded curve of his ass. Just beneath, she saw his ball sack swing. Carmen licked her lips, wondering just how soft it was, and just how delicious it would feel between her lips. Her body, recently denied its climax, responded immediately. She imagined pulling that velvety skin between his legs into her mouth and sucking ever-so-gently. His erection would grow harder and harder, she knew, but she'd wait to suck on that until they were both good and ready. Carmen loved nothing more than the pure tactile pleasure of a steel-hard male organ in her mouth, and it had been far, far too long since she'd indulged.

"Aha!" he crowed. "Organic goats' cheese!" He straightened, beaming with delight, and looked like a chenille-clad combination of Hugh Grant and Johnny Depp. Somehow, the mash-up worked gloriously well. Carmen moved her eyes down the front of the fuzzy peach robe, gaping open at his broad chest, to the loosely tied belt, then to the micro-mini hemline. Just under the edge of the hem, she saw the soft pink tip of his penis sway tantalisingly. She took a deep breath to clear her thoughts.

"Yes, that's great stuff, made locally." She stood. "I'll get some crackers. We might as well have a snack, right?" The bizarreness of the situation was overwhelming. At least cheese and crackers would add a touch of reality to this night. Carmen arranged some crackers on a plate along with the cheese and a knife. She placed the plate along with a napkin for each of them on the kitchen table and sat down with her tea. "Won't you join me, Brock?"

"Don't mind if I do," he answered. Rubbing his broad hands together with the delight of a kid at Christmastime, he sat in front of her at the table and began to dig in. He seemed oblivious to the fact that the robe split open when he spread his knees to sit—it exposed every sumptuous bit of his package. Carmen knew there was no way she could sit with him and ignore the sight of his thick shaft folded cosily against his balls.

"Ahem." Carmen cleared her throat. "That robe's not really working out for you or, ah, me. Let me see if I've got some sweatpants you can wear."

"Oh, sorry," Brock replied. "How's this?"

Carmen gaped. He was now fully dressed in knee length cargo shorts, hiking sandals, and a snug black V-neck T-shirt. "Better?" Brock asked. He helped himself to a hunk of cheese on top of a cracker.

"Oh my God!" Carmen sputtered. "Is this like the cat thing?"

Brock nodded, his mouth full of goats' cheese and buttery cracker. He took a sip of tea and pointed his finger at Carmen. "Bingo! It's exactly like that. A glamour, Carmen. I'm still wearing your robe, which is very comfy by the way, but your eyes are telling you that I'm wearing these clothes instead."

Carmen scrunched her eyebrows in confusion. She brought one hand to the hem of his shorts, but her fingers passed straight through the fabric. Instead, she found herself stroking his thigh—tautly muscled and dusted with soft hair. Reflexively, Carmen gave his leg an appreciative squeeze before blushing and pulling her hand away. "So, you're still actually wearing my robe?"

"Yup," Brock concurred matter-of-factly. "What you see is just a glamour."

"Well, it's a pretty cool trick," Carmen said. "I wish I could do it. Does the glamour hold for everybody else? Like, if somebody else walked into this room, would they see you in these clothes or in my old bathrobe?"

"Good question," Brock answered. He took a moment to chew another bite of cracker and chase it with some mint tea. "It would depend on whether that person has any magic. More specifically, it would depend on how much magic that person has. For example, some humans have a little trace of magic in them naturally. Say their great-great-grandma got it on with an elf or something. These things happen, you know." Carmen chuckled. "They might see something funny or shimmery about the clothes I'm wearing, but they'd still see them. And some magic beings experience the world differently than others. Trolls, for instance, are all about brawn and not so much about brains. Their magic has less finesse than elves, for instance. Trolls probably would see both the robe and the clothes, but they wouldn't care much. They'd be more interested in your chickens out back, frankly."

"Trolls," Carmen replied drily. "You're telling me there are trolls out there?"

"Not so many as before," Brock conceded, "but sure, there are trolls. Even trolls, though, have a built-in glamour about them as sort of a self-protection. To your eyes, they'd probably appear as bears. Which works out fine, since both trolls and bears are best avoided by humans. Plus, both tend to have horrible breath. And don't even get me started on gnome halitosis."

"Uh-huh."

"Trolls, elves, tree spirits, gnomes, you name it. Prescott Woods is home to all sorts of magical creatures. Some were born that way, while others transformed for one reason or another, but all share that same ingredient—magic."

"Right," Carmen said. "Including you, right, Brock?" Brock again made a 'Bingo!' gesture and scarfed down another cracker. "And you're, what, an elf? A gnome?" Carmen asked.

Brock took a swig of tea before answering. "I am one of the Fair Folk," he informed her.

"You're, like, a fairy?" Carmen suppressed a giggle. The tall, golden-brown, luxuriantly muscled man before her was about as far from her idea of a fairy as, well, a big grey tomcat.

"I'm one of the Fair Folk," he corrected her, "and I live in Prescott Woods, which is in imminent danger, as I'm sure you know."

Carmen nodded. "I know. I'm really bummed about it, but I'm not sure what I can do to stop the development. How did you hear about it? Little gnome spies, perhaps?"

Brock chuckled. "No need for little gnome spies. My glamour is very helpful for eavesdropping. I'm sure you can imagine."

Carmen humphed and helped herself to a cracker with cheese.

Brock continued, "Old Man Prescott, after all these years, came into the woods with some business types. They talked about chopping down the trees, laying water pipes and electrical wires, and building luxury homes for rich folks."

"Yes, I'd heard pretty much the same thing. The thought of Prescott Woods being demolished is upsetting, but the laid-back nature of Charade being lost is just unthinkable. But it's Prescott's land, right? What can we do to stop him?"

After guzzling the remainder of his herbal tea, Brock fixed her with his arresting sapphire blue eyes. "Calvin Prescott, like his father, grandfather, great-grandfather, great-great-grandfather, and great-great-great-grandfather, does *not* own the woods. He, like his forebears, is simply a caretaker. The Fair Folk — specifically, my family — own both the woods and the Prescott house. About two hundred years ago, my father had Prescott Manor built. He allowed the Prescott family to live there with the understanding that they would maintain the secrecy and safety of Prescott Woods. Old Man Prescott, apparently, has decided to renege on his family's vow. We're not going to stand for that."

Carmen tried to concentrate on his words, but his body was more than a little distracting. She watched his face, transfixed. He ground his jaw in anger and his bronzed cheekbones jutted out like blades. Brock's wild grey hair stood up on end, but, instead of making him look older, it gave glorious contrast to his smooth, warm brown skin. Carmen blushed, thinking that, although he appeared to be fully dressed in shorts and T-shirt, Brock was fully exposed in front of her.

Carmen looked up from his crotch and caught him staring at her, amusement glittering in his eyes. "Come here, Carmen," he said as he stood. "They're not going to chop down the woods in the next hour. I want to show you something." He took her hand and led her back to her bedroom.

Chapter Five

Carmen's pulse raced when he shut the door behind them. She didn't know if it was terror or wild desire coursing through her, but she was dizzy with excitement from one or the other. Brock took a pillow from her bed and placed it on the floor in front of his feet. At once, the glamour melted away from him and he was clad in her short robe once more. Brock untied it and tossed it away. Carmen swallowed with difficulty. A gorgeous, shining erection sprang from his groin. Carmen caught the faintest whiff of musk from him—woodsy, earthy, and green-sweet like new grass. She watched, frozen with lust, as he took the huge organ in his fist and pumped it slowly. "You keep looking at it, Carmen," he whispered. "Don't you want to taste it?"

Carmen's mouth fell open. A million reasons why *not* flickered through her mind like a shuffling deck of cards. *It's not what nice girls do, you don't even know this man, he's a peeping tom, he's far too presumptuous, he might be dangerous...*

Then she looked back down. A clear drop of pre-cum had escaped from the tip of his shaft. It slickened the ruddy round head as he moved his hand over it. She salivated, desperate to know just how delicious he would taste.

As in a trance, Carmen dropped to her knees on the pillow before him. She lifted her hand to his erection. Oh, God, it was just as steel-hard as she'd hoped. She cupped his balls in her hand, savouring their weight. Although she was ravenous for his cock, Carmen wanted to sample his balls first. She gripped his length in her hand, pumping it slowly, and lowered her face to his sac.

She traced her tongue over the loose skin, nibbling it between her lips then opened her mouth wider to suck in one plump testicle. It filled her mouth and dominated her senses. He tasted masculine and vital. It was everything she'd been missing for the past five years. Well, almost.

She released his testicle from her mouth, giving the skin of his sac one final, appreciative kiss, and turned her attention to his erection. Carmen licked the slit in its tip. The flavour of his semen spread across her tongue like a melting cube of sugar. Delicious. Intoxicating.

Brock ran his fingers over her scalp as she drew him into her mouth. His cock grew thicker between her lips. Carmen gripped his rear to pull him closer. The firm curves of his ass cheeks bunched beneath her fingers. He plunged into her mouth, silent and intent.

Carmen's mouth watered like that of a starving animal. Her mouth filled with saliva, encasing Brock's shaft in a wet sheath. She swallowed, tongue and lips moving rhythmically, and Brock grunted. Carmen pulled his hips towards her face faster, feeding his length into her mouth at a greater speed. Brock gave a feral shout as his orgasm overtook him. He pumped his shaft into Carmen's mouth, using two fistfuls of her hair to hold her head in place. His grip was entirely unnecessary, though. Carmen was deliriously aroused and was savouring every yummy drop that he gave her.

Carmen slid her hands between Brock's legs, letting her fingers glide over the lightly furred skin of his thighs. She suckled appreciatively as his orgasm wound down. He released his tight hold on her hair and ran his fingers down the side of her face. "That was fabulous, Carmen. Damn, woman, that felt good."

Carmen let his softening penis slide wetly from her mouth. "It was my pleasure, I assure you." She planted a kiss on the tender skin of his upper thigh and stood. Going down on Brock had fired up every nerve in her body—the crotch of her jeans was clammy and damp with her juices. Dressed in her bulky navy sweatshirt as well, Carmen felt entirely too clothed as she ran her hands down the warm skin of Brock's ribs and hips. "From peeping tomcat to blow job recipient in one night," she whispered, and licked the sticky corners of her mouth. "I'd say you're doing pretty good, Brock."

"But I'm not done yet," he informed her. He slipped her sweatshirt over her head in one quick movement. Carmen blushed to feel the cool air on her exposed breasts. A pesky voice in the back of her mind fretted, *You don't know this guy!* Carmen shooed it away with ease, choosing to focus on the glorious sight before her eyes. *I know that he looks, tastes and feels divine, and that it'll do me no good whatsoever to call the cops.*

"Five years, huh, Carmen?" Brock noted. He unbuttoned her jeans and shoved them down to her ankles before lifting her feet, one at a time, to free her from the heavy denim. "That's way too long, lovely."

He pressed his broad, warm chest against hers, letting the tight nubs of her tits rub against his smooth skin. Shifting his hips against hers, Brock rubbed his semi-erect cock against Carmen's belly. He took her breasts in his hands and kneaded them. Carmen felt the soft inner walls of her cunt melt when he lowered his face to suckle one nipple. "Oh, God," she murmured.

Brock eased her against the foot of the bed and cupped his hand between her legs. "You're so wet," he said, his voice muffled by his mouthful of her flesh.

Carmen's knees felt weak and she was grateful to have the edge of the bed propping her up. She wondered idly if she'd have a hickey or two by the time this was over. Carmen gasped with pain and surprise when he bit her nipple between his sharp teeth, then sighed when he covered the offended breast with his soothing, wet mouth.

He eased his fingers into her pussy - pushing one, then two, then three inside her. Carmen's body thrummed with energy. She bucked her hips against his hand, and cried out when he brought the pad of his thumb to her clit. "Mmm-hmm," she murmured, "that's good."

Brock lifted his face from her reddened, swollen breast. Not missing a beat with his finger-fucking, he lifted his other hand to the side of her face. "You're so beautiful, Carmen," he told her, "in every way I can see." Carmen's pussy contracted around his fingers, sending a fresh torrent of her juices running down his hand. Brock eased his other hand behind her neck, holding her as though she were made of crystal.

"I haven't kissed you yet," he whispered, "but I've wanted to. I've watched you sleeping, and watched you in the mornings when you wake up and touch yourself. I've watched you dancing at the rec centre, and wanted to rush into the room and take you right there." He traced circles with his thumb over her clit. "I've watched you care for your animals. I've watched you do your law work, and I've watched you bag vegetables at the food co-op." He lowered his face to hers so that Carmen felt the warm, moist puffs of air from his mouth.

Inside her, he found her G-spot with his fingertip. Carmen closed her eyes and thrust her hips against his palm, begging for more of the contact.

His lips brushed against hers, softly and reverently. Carmen felt her orgasm move like the flow of lava from a volcano—from her weeping pussy, to her swollen, sensitive tits, and finally to her mouth, where it bloomed like a firework.

She cried out, but her shout was muted by his lips on hers. He filled her mouth with his tongue, mimicking the methodical fucking that his hand was giving her cunt. Carmen fell limp against the foot of the bed as her climax throbbed through her body. Brock kept his fingers deep inside her until her last spasm ended.

When Carmen opened her eyes, she saw Brock's satisfied face before her. "Was it worth the wait?" he asked.

Carmen laughed shakily. "It was amazing," she answered, "although I sure don't want to wait another five years before it happens again."

Cock-a-doodle-doooo!

Carmen realised that, in the midst of the first sex she'd had in half a decade, the first rays of sunlight had crept over the countryside. "That would be Spare Tire," she told Brock, "greeting the dawn."

Carmen gloried in the gorgeous tactile sensation of his nude body pressed against hers and the tender kisses he placed on the side of her neck. "What do you say we get cleaned up," Brock offered, "and I show you where I live in the woods?"

"Ah." Carmen nodded. She cupped her hands around his sculpted ass cheeks and traced her fingers down the crease between them. "And where do the Fair Folk live, anyway? In toadstool rings glamoured up to look like condos? Maybe a glamoured cave that looks like a posh hotel?"

"Erm, no. What I'll show you is the real deal, no glamour involved," Brock told her. "You have to understand that you can't ever tell anyone about it. Not that it would matter, though—"

"Right, because if I brought anyone out to see it, they'd see, like, a big pile of firewood or something."

"Exactly," Brock confirmed. "And, Carmen, do you think we could maybe bring some of your eggs to the homestead? We don't have any chickens, and the eggs you have are free-range..."

Carmen chuckled. "By all means, Brock. Let's save you the trouble of stealing any more." She thought she saw the faintest trace of a blush beneath his deeply tanned cheeks. "And yes, I'd be happy to bring some eggs in exchange for a visit to the Fair Folk's home in the woods."

Chapter Six

An hour later, Carmen set off behind Brock into the murky twilight of Prescott Woods. Although only few steps separated her backyard from the lush old growth of trees, it seemed a world away. Another hour of picking their way among gnarled roots and craggy terrain brought them deep into the lush interior of the woods.

"So, you're telling me that there are magical beings in here, like elves and trolls and who-knows-what? And that I won't even be able to see them as they are?" Carmen shuddered. She shifted her backpack — loaded with a few just-in-case necessities and a dozen carefully packed eggs — on her shoulders.

"Don't worry," Brock reassured her. He gallantly lifted a thorny branch from her path and held it as she walked by. "They may well show their true selves when they see that I'm with you, but you will definitely not be in danger as long as you're with me."

"What, you'll glamour yourself into a squirrel and chuck nuts at them?" Carmen muttered as she stepped past him.

Brock chuckled. "That's always an option, if worst comes to worst. But I don't think it will be necessary. My clan, the Fair Folk, rule these woods. Even the dark magic folk would only harm us if we attacked them first." He caught Carmen's elbow and stopped her. "Look, I know you only just met me, but you can trust me, Carmen. I'm inviting you to my home because I think you can help us save it, and also because I admire you." He wrapped one strong arm around the small of her back and pulled her tightly to him in a stomach-to-stomach hold. "And because I am growing increasingly fond of you, minute by minute."

Carmen heard the rustle of woodland animals and the screeching call of a bird. The woods whirled away from her, though—all that mattered was the wild man in front of her. She raised her hands to his sides and was immediately reminded that his clothing—the hiking shorts and T-shirt—were simply a glamour. His warm, bare skin slid beneath her hands. Lower, at her stomach, he pressed his exposed cock insistently into her flesh. Pinpricks of arousal sparked at her breasts and in the slick space between her thighs.

"And because I desire you as I've never desired any woman." He lowered his face to hers for a deep, lingering kiss.

Carmen melted against his tall frame. Had a man's touch ever felt this sublime? She opened her mouth to his flickering tongue and traced her hands down the taut muscles of his lower back to the crease of his rear. Carmen grazed her fingernails over the delicate skin from his asshole to his balls as she twirled her tongue against his. Brock growled and pulled her closer, deepening his kiss.

"Ahem," a female voice interrupted.

Carmen broke the kiss and pulled away, her cheeks flaming. She saw a young woman with thick tangles of fiery orange hair that fell nearly to her waist. She wore a simple strapless wrap dress that fell nearly to her knees. The tan linen was plain, but it hugged her lithe, athletic figure perfectly. Her feet were bare, and she wore a mocking expression.

"What's she doing here, Brock?" the woman spat. "You need to get her out of here, immediately, and even then, Father may decide she knows too much." Her black eyes glinted angrily.

"Carmen, please meet my sister, Paloma. I apologise for her coarse manners. Paloma, may I introduce my friend, Carmen?" Brock placed a protective arm around Carmen as he spoke.

Paloma ignored Carmen and focused her wrath on Brock. "Again I ask, brother, what is this woman doing here? You know that outsiders are not allowed."

Brock sighed. "I had hoped to speak to Father before I ran into you or Lowell," he explained. "You know that the woods are in trouble. Carmen can help us. She loves Charade and is opposed to the planned development. She's also a lawyer with lots of friends in town."

Paloma ran her eyes up and down Carmen's frame before glaring back at Brock. "It doesn't hurt that you find her attractive, though, does it? You're so predictable."

Carmen heard footsteps on the crunchy woodland floor. A whitetail buck stepped slowly towards them. It stopped just a foot away from Carmen and Brock, its nostrils flaring with each breath. Carmen's eyes widened at the sight of the beautiful creature standing so close to her. In the blink of an eye, the deer vanished and a bearded man stood in its place.

He was massive and tall. He reminded Carmen of the flannel-clad woodsman on the Brawny paper towel packages. Like the Brawny man she remembered from her girlhood, this guy sported tousled brown hair, faded red plaid flannel shirt and blue jeans. Vintage Tom Selleck with an edge and a beard, she decided at once.

"Explain this, Brock," the man demanded in a deep rumble. "Explain why you have brought this mortal woman here." He studied Carmen with all the compassion of a hungry shark.

"Father, I wanted to speak to you at our home. Carmen can help us save the woods. She can—"

"Silence!" the man boomed. The sounds of calling birds and rustling creatures ended at once. The entire woods seemed intimidated by the burly patriarch. "You meant to bring her to Speranza?" His eyes narrowed angrily. "To our family's home, Brock?"

"Yes, sir, I did," Brock answered calmly.

The great man held one hand up for silence. "Very well, then. Escort her to Speranza. Do not take her back to her house. We will discuss the matter as a family. Paloma, please summon Lowell and Korbin."

Paloma nodded to her father, smirked at Brock, then darted off into the woods. Brock's father gave Carmen a passing glance before addressing Brock once more. "You should know," he told him, "that there's no going back now, Brock. You've sealed this mortal woman's fate. If our family remains unconvinced that we have a need for her, then I'm afraid that's the end of it. Regardless, she is, under no circumstances, to leave the woods without my clearance."

At that, Brock's father strode off through the woods. Brock watched his form disappear into the trees.

Carmen waited long moments for him to speak, then couldn't wait another second. "Listen, Brock, what did he mean by, 'that's the end of it'? What's that all about?"

Brock took her hand and kissed it. "It's going to be okay, Carmen. Our woods are in real danger, and I believe you are our best bet to save them." His intense blue eyes crinkled as he smiled. "And like Paloma said, it doesn't hurt that I find you attractive."

"Look, I love the woods, too, and I love Charade, but I don't want to be, like, turned into a stump or something if your family doesn't like me. Let's just go back, okay?"

"I'm sorry, Carmen, but that's no longer an option," Brock replied. "Father knows you're here, and he controls every part of Prescott Woods. If we tried to leave without speaking with my family, they would find us before we could reach your backyard. And they'd be even more suspicious of you." He began to lead her deeper into the woods.

Carmen followed him in silence, alternately listening to the voices of fear and curiosity that argued in her mind. She and Brock stopped at a fallen tree for a rest and some bottled water. As they passed the cool spring water back and forth, Brock gave Carmen a briefing about his family. "They're great, really, but we all have our quirks," he told her. "Father's name is Gavin Rossi. He found this place when we were still kids and we settled here. Mother died while Korbin was being born, and, as soon as Korbin was old enough to travel, Father left New York and headed south to seek his fortune with us kids in tow. Of course, that was a really long time ago."

Brock cleared his throat and continued, "Lowell is my oldest brother. He's most like Father, I suppose, but a bit more hot-tempered. A real might-means-right kind of guy when he's cornered. Paloma is the next oldest. I'm not sure why, but for the last several decades she's grown increasingly bitter and unforgiving. She used to be so playful. We were the closest siblings when we were growing up. Korbin is the youngest of us, and the most studious, too. He's fascinated by woodland lore and herbal healing, that sort of thing. Sometimes he needs a good shake to get him going when there's a crisis, but he's a good sort."

"Mm-hmm." Carmen nodded. "I hear you, but I'm still stuck on what you said about Paloma. For the last several decades she's been cranky? She doesn't look older than twenty-five, Brock! And your father looks no older than you do. Is that part of the glamour you guys can do?"

"No, glamour has nothing to do with it. The way you see him now, and the way you saw Father, Paloma, and the rest of us, is exactly how our bodies naturally appear. Once we reach adulthood, we don't age, Carmen. And Father's body actually grew younger in appearance when we obtained our magic. Although, we can use our glamour to appear older or younger if the mood strikes us, of course," he concluded.

They capped the water bottle and set off once more. Carmen's home seemed a world away. She wondered idly what Spare Tire was up to, and if the shaky truce between him and Dax was still holding up. Finally, Brock announced, "We're almost there, Carmen."

"Thank goodness," Carmen breathed. "At this point, I'm almost ready to be turned into a stump just so I can rest. My legs are shaking from all this up and down movement."

Brock's mouth quirked devilishly. "I'd much rather your legs be shaking from a different sort of up and down movement, but, with luck, we can work that out later today."

Carmen's cheeks flamed with embarrassed excitement. A little up-down movement with Brock sounded like the perfect reward for this hike, if, that is, she survived the Fair Folk family interview. She trailed Brock for another few yards before the woods opened up into an enormous clearing.

Carmen looked up, shook her head, squinted and looked again. "A castle? In the middle of the woods? For real, is this another glamour, Brock?"

"Nope," he assured her. "This is the real deal. Welcome to Castle Speranza, Carmen." Carmen's eyes drank in the elegant limestone structure. Four conical-roofed towers graced each corner of the three-storey castle. Narrow arched windows, largest on the bottom floor and smallest on top, dotted the grey stone walls. The woods encroached close to the castle's lawn, which was more a great patch of wild violets than an actual grassy lawn. Carmen caught the glimmer of a wide pond that extended beyond the left wall of the structure, complete with pink water lilies. She smiled to see a mama wood duck, with six little masked ducklings in tow, waddle past her feet and towards the sparkling expanse of water behind the castle.

Paloma emerged from the woods flanked by two men. Carmen could see a slight family resemblance between the brothers, but they were polar opposites in appearance. Paloma halted, scowling, and crossed her arms.

"Carmen," Brock said, "allow me to introduce my other siblings. This is Lowell, my older brother." He gestured towards a solidly built man with a head full of shaggy raven-black hair and a heavy jaw dotted with stubble. He looked, Carmen decided, an awful lot like his father, minus the beard and with extra snarl.

Carmen forced a weak smile and held her hand out for a handshake. Lowell flicked his eyes at her outstretched palm and glowered. "Carmen, huh?" he growled. Coffee-brown eyes squinted beneath his full black eyebrows. "I hope you enjoy your visit to Castle Speranza, Carmen," he grumbled, "because it's going to be the last thing you remember." Lowell flexed his fingers and balled them into fists.

"Now, now, Lowell, no need to get all gloom and doom on us." Brock chuckled uncomfortably. "We're just talking here. I'm sure that once you understand what Carmen has to offer, you'll be grateful she's here."

Carmen tried to squash the panic rising in her throat. What the hell had Brock got her into?

"And Carmen, this is my younger brother, Korbin," Brock continued. Korbin was tall, thin, and graceful-looking. Above clear green eyes, he sported a mane of fine, white-blond hair. Korbin gave Carmen a soft smile and reached for a handshake. His grip felt warm and strong in her hand.

"Hi, Carmen," Korbin said. "Don't let Lowell and Paloma scare you. I'm sure Brock wouldn't have brought you here without good reason." Lowell cut a fierce glare at Korbin, who coloured slightly, but held his gaze.

Brock's father opened the front door of the castle. "All here?" he asked in a deep voice. "Good. Come in, all of you." He disappeared into the imposing structure. Brock squeezed Carmen's hand, now slippery with anxious sweat, and led her inside after Paloma.

Chapter Seven

Even with the fear of death or stump-transformation looming, Carmen was dazzled by Castle Speranza's interior. It was opulent, gorgeous, gleaming — everything a fairy tale castle should be. Oriental rugs covered rich wood floors and enormous crystal chandeliers glittered overhead. *How in the world did they get electricity out here?* Carmen wondered. Ornately carved furniture, much of it marble-topped, graced every part of the home she could see, and heavy gilt mirrors hung on the walls. Carmen craned her neck to see the fabulous double staircase with its lavish wrought iron balusters. She could almost make out the design in the jewel-toned stained glass window at the landing —

"A-hem!" Paloma cleared her throat abruptly. She stood in the wide doorway to the library in front of soaring walls of leather bound books and wheeled library ladders. Paloma made a sweeping come-inside gesture and said, in a voice dripping with scorn, "If you're quite done gaping, would you please grace us with your company? It's not like we have anything else to do today, and, after all, we've been expecting you. Oh, wait!" Paloma added, appearing to enjoy delivering her barbed words. "We didn't expect you at all, did we? And we don't actually want you here, either."

"Enough!" Gavin bellowed from his great armchair at the oval library table. "Brock, please direct your friend to a seat." Brock gave Carmen's hand one more squeeze and showed her to a red velvet padded chair. Paloma took the chair to Gavin's left, and Lowell was already seated at his right. Casting her eyes at Paloma, then Gavin, then Lowell, Carmen saw shades of scorn, haughtiness, and animosity. At least Korbin seemed friendly, Carmen noted. He smiled at her as she and Brock sat down.

An expectant silence fell over the room. Gavin spoke first. "Brock, you know as well as any of us that we do not bring mortals into Prescott Woods. We do not reveal our true natures, along with those of other magical creatures, to humans, even on those rare occasions when we have a dalliance with a mortal." Lowell's cheeks reddened and he looked down at his lap. "Above all" — Gavin's voice grew angrier — "we do not bring mortals to Castle Speranza." Brock studied his clasped hands. "These laws are not only for your own safety, they are for the safety of every magical creature in these woods." He fixed his soft grey eyes on Brock and waited for his reply. "Explain yourself, son."

Brock took Carmen's hand underneath the table. He smiled at her, sapphire eyes gleaming then turned to Gavin. "Carmen knows about Calvin Prescott's plans for the woods," he told his father. "She cares about the woods, and she cares about Charade. She doesn't want to see the trees get mowed down and replaced by a bunch of mansions and a horde of new residents."

"Humph," Lowell grunted. "And so what? I'm sure there are plenty of Charade residents who feel the same way."

"Yes, well, Carmen is also a lawyer," Brock continued. "She worked in a posh firm in Chicago before relocating to Charade, and she still practises law. She could help us find a way to legally stop Calvin Prescott from selling the land."

"Pah!" Paloma spat. "We don't need a legal way to stop him! I've got a way that's a lot simpler and faster, and it involves a switchblade and one quick slice." Her black eyes glittered.

Gavin raised one hand for silence. "Continue, Brock."

"Well, Carmen has a lot of friends in Charade who might help us, too," he said.

"Help us what?" Lowell laughed. "Argue with Old Man Prescott that trees are worth more than money to him? I say we let them try to take a single tree in Prescott Woods down. They'll rue the day, I promise you." Lowell cracked his knuckles. "Between us and the trolls and the gnomes, not to mention the tree spirits, who'll be fighting for their lives, we'll make anyone wielding a chain saw wish he'd never woken up that day."

"We don't have to fight!" Korbin interjected. "We could let them take part of the woods, just the outside part, and leave the interior to us. The tree spirits only live in the interior, you know. We could let them have a good third of the woods, with the understanding that they'll never touch the rest of it."

"Bah!" Gavin shouted and banged his fist on the table. "You know the greed of mortals, son! They would never be content with just a piece of Prescott Woods. Once we give way one little bit, they will never rest until the entire woods are gone and we are homeless and as good as dead."

"If I may speak," Carmen offered hesitantly, "since it is, after all, my own fate you're trying to determine, I have to say that I agree with Gavin. If a partial development of Prescott Woods is successful, Calvin Prescott will feel a great deal of pressure to sell the rest of it."

Gavin nodded and gestured for Carmen to continue. "With respect, Paloma," she went on, "I think that killing Calvin Prescott will hardly eliminate the problem of the proposed development. As far as anyone in town knows, Calvin Prescott has no close relatives. If his will dictates that his property will go to a distant cousin or to a charity, it's quite likely that the beneficiary will want to see the proposed development to its completion and reap the financial rewards. Someone who doesn't even live in Charade would be even more likely to value money over trees."

Paloma shot eye daggers at Carmen in reply.

"And Lowell, while I certainly understand your frustration, I feel that an assault on the workers will also not give you the result you want. If there appear to be wild animals or even spirits in the woods, I feel confident that investigations will follow, one after the other, until the forest yields up all its secrets. Of course, if every investigator is attacked, the property owner, be it Calvin Prescott or whoever he wants to sell the land to, will need to resort to drastic measures to clear the trees. Fire, maybe, or perhaps a bunch of guys with guns and grenades. Who knows? They're not going to let a wood full of dangerous and mysterious creatures just sit there, though."

Lowell's bushy black eyebrows knotted over his warm brown eyes.

"I do feel, however, that we can save Prescott Woods from destruction. I think the path starts with Calvin Prescott. Perhaps it ends with a liberal dose of Fair Folk glamour, who knows? I can take care of any legal entanglements as well as enlisting the aid of news media, if it comes to that. I'm sure the evening news would love to show a bunch of small-town protestors whose way of life is threatened by big-money developers."

Gavin nodded. "Your plan is to trick Calvin Prescott in some manner to leave the woods as is, even though he knows, as do we all, that his family is honour-bound to keep Prescott Woods intact regardless?"

"I suppose," said Carmen. "But I can also look at the legal ramifications here, including quality of life for Charade residents and zoning, to try to stop him."

"I see." He leant back in his chair. "Well, I think we've heard quite enough. I, for one, am unconvinced that glamour is the answer here. I feel that Lowell's idea of repelling the construction crew by any means necessary is the course of action that is most likely to lead to success, and that you, Carmen, are both unwelcome and unnecessary. Lowell, are you in agreement?"

Lowell nodded grimly. "I am."

"And you, Paloma?" Gavin turned to his fiery-haired daughter.

"Oh, yes, Father," Paloma agreed, "we hardly need this mortal woman here at Castle Speranza. Although I may still steal into Old Man Prescott's house just to see if a terrible and fatal accident has occurred" — she smiled wickedly — "or is about to occur."

Brock began to sputter in protest, but Gavin raised his hand to silence him. "I'm sure we all know your opinions on the matter, Brock," he stated. "Korbin? How do you weigh in, son?"

Korbin coughed and looked around the table at Paloma, Gavin, Lowell, Brock, and, finally, Carmen. "I think Carmen's right," he said at last. "I don't want Prescott Woods to be cut down, any of it. I think that using a glamour on Old Man Prescott is worth a shot. If that fails, perhaps Carmen's legal expertise can serve us."

"That's it, then," Gavin stated with finality. "Lowell, Paloma and myself are opposed to Carmen's presence and aid. Brock and Korbin are in favour of it." His voice took on the gravity of an executioner. "As I said before, Brock, this will be the end of it. Lowell, please ensure that Carmen never leaves these woods and never remembers anything about her life prior to today."

The colour drained from Brock's face. "Father, no! I brought her here and told her she'd be safe. Please, you must reconsider!"

"You were wrong to do so," Lowell said, "though I doubt that you'll ever make this mistake again. You must keep your dalliances with mortals in their world, and leave them behind before you come home. You know that, Brock, as do Paloma, Korbin and I."

Lowell walked to Carmen's chair and grabbed her upper arm in a vice-like grip. "Come with me," he demanded.

Carmen was dizzy with terror. "No, no, you can't do this!" she shouted. "I can really help you!" Lowell lifted her to her feet. "If I don't go home, then who will teach my belly-dancing classes? Who will feed Dax, my Labrador?" Lowell started to pull her towards the library door. "And who will feed my chickens?" Carmen sobbed. "They'll all starve without me."

"Wait just a minute!" shouted Paloma. "Did you say chickens?" Carmen nodded miserably.

"Is this where you've been getting those eggs?" Paloma asked Brock. He gave his affirmation. "Well, then," Paloma declared, "I change my vote, Father."

"What's this?" Gavin blustered. "You're changing your vote because she owns chickens?" His broad face grew red with anger.

"I'm changing my vote," she clarified, "because her chickens lay fabulous eggs, Father, and we don't have any chickens here. Were Carmen to relocate to Castle Speranza and bring her fowl with her, I feel that she would be a lovely addition to our home."

Gavin stared at her in incredulity.

"And who knows," Paloma added, "maybe she can figure out a way to trick Old Man Prescott into living up to his family's side of the bargain. Gaia knows I don't care about him," she snorted, "but I would hate for any of us to be hurt defending Prescott Woods."

Lowell's grip loosened on Carmen's upper arm. "I wasn't going to say anything," he muttered, "but, Father, you know I've always wanted a dog."

"What?" Gavin bellowed. "Are you changing your vote because she has a dog?"

Lowell suddenly expressed a great interest in his shoes.

"And what about you, Korbin?" grumbled Gavin. "Are you going to tell me you've always had a hankering to take belly dancing lessons?"

Korbin grinned. "None for me, Father," he answered, "but you never know, perhaps even those skills will come in handy."

"Well then," Gavin boomed. He stood, massive and furious. "I see that I am outvoted by every one of my children. Keep her here, then, Brock, for now. Until I am convinced of her loyalty and discretion, she is not to leave this place. Am I understood?"

"Yes, Father," Brock agreed.

"And Brock, I do not need to remind you of the rules of Castle Speranza, do I?" he asked. "I put my trust in you."

"That's as it should be, Father," Brock replied.

"And what of the chickens?" asked Paloma.

"And the dog?" Lowell added.

"Argghhh!" Gavin threw his hands into the air. "Go get the damn chickens and the thrice-damned dog," he barked. "What do I care? Turn Castle Speranza into a zoo, right under my feet. After all, I'm just the one who built it—what does my opinion matter?" Gavin stalked out of the room and to the front door. "Retrieve the animals and we will discuss the matter of Calvin Prescott," his voice thundered from the porch as he exited.

"Right, then," Paloma said cheerfully. "Let's go get my chickens!"

"And don't forget my dog!" Lowell added.

"Excuse me," Carmen insisted. "I appreciate very much that you all voted to keep me around instead of whatever vile thing you had in mind, but I'll remind you that they are *my* chickens"—she gave Paloma a meaningful glare—"and *my* dog," Carmen informed Lowell. "Although," she acquiesced, "I am certainly willing to share them."

Chapter Eight

As they journeyed with Paloma and Lowell to fetch Dax, the chickens and Spare Tire, Carmen learnt more of the history of Prescott Woods.

"When Father arrived at Charade, it wasn't much more than a trading post and a flea-infested inn," Brock told her. "To him, though, it seemed perfect. He wanted nothing more than an escape from New York City and the consumption that had claimed Mother's life. He wanted to take us where we could never get sick. He promised Mother on her deathbed that he would protect us."

Lowell grunted in agreement. "You were just seven then, Brock," he added, "but old enough to understand what was happening. It was a terrible time. Paloma and I were frightened, but of course we had to obey Father and leave everything we knew in the city."

"We were still children ourselves," added Paloma, "but I was ten and old enough to watch the wee ones while Father searched for our new home. Lowell was twelve, but already as tall as a man, so he guarded the rest of us."

Brock took Carmen's hand to steady her as she picked her way across the raised stones in a bubbling stream. "At the Charade Inn, Father heard rumours of the haunted woods," Brock continued. "It seemed that no one was brave enough to venture into the woods for fear of evil spirits and strange monsters. To Father, it was perfect! No one would trouble us if we settled in a place they were afraid to approach, and he thought all the talk of supernatural beings was nonsense. Father left the four of us with the innkeeper, Mack Prescott, and his wife when he went to explore the woods."

Korbin said, "We can't imagine what Father encountered. Prescott Woods was, and is, full of beings far removed from the world of man. At that time, they were disorganised and leaderless, but Father must have encountered a troll or two, and elves can be vicious about traps and snares."

"Three long days passed," Lowell continued. "As the oldest, I worried nonstop while he was gone. What if he never returned at all? Where would we go? Mack Prescott and his wife were nice enough, but they were hardly prepared to take in four kids permanently. When Father came limping up to the Charade Inn, I felt the weight of the world lift from my shoulders."

Paloma chuckled. "Father looked like he'd been dragged through a briar patch and over a cliff by a team of wild horses. He was elated, though. There was a hopeful excitement about him that had been missing ever since Mother died. I still remember what he said then, 'Come, children. Bring your things. I will settle with the innkeep. I have found our new home.' We followed him through the woods. We heard frightening, inhuman sounds all around us, but Father was fearless. 'I am the master of these woods now,' he told us, 'for I have bested all creatures who dared to fight me. The beings here have pledged their loyalty to me and are at my command.'"

"We saw the proof of Father's new status as soon as we reached the camp," Brock stated. "There were four small, bent women — gnomes, we learnt — ready to wait on us. Gnome men had constructed a wooden home for us next to the opening to the bathing cavern. We stayed in that wooden home while Castle Speranza was built and Father hammered out the details of his arrangement with Mack Prescott."

"It must have taken ages," Carmen noted. "Digging, cutting and placing all those rocks are monumental jobs."

"True," answered Brock, "but we had a few things going for us. Father had a framed drawing of Acqua Dolce castle near Padua, Italy. Mother grew up near the castle and always loved it. She kept the drawing after she and Father married and crossed the Atlantic. Father gave the drawing to the gnomes, who are skilled, tireless workers. With the help of some trolls, who were also obedient to Father's will, the castle work went quickly. In just a few months, our new home was ready for us."

"But what about all those furnishings?" Carmen asked. "The chandeliers, the rugs, the furniture, the paintings, the mirrors..."

Brock shrugged. "Magical beings are, well, magical, Carmen. After the structure was built, Father called on the elves for the interior work. Fine carving, weaving, artwork — they're good at that sort of thing."

"It's pretty remarkable that your father was able to enlist their help. Did they resent it?"

"It was in the magical beings' best interest, too," Lowell interjected. "They didn't have a ruler, and historically had been unable to abide by a creature of a different sort giving them orders. That is, the elves wouldn't tolerate a gnome ruler, and the tree spirits would never put up with a troll bossing them about. The woods were in a constant state of battle and confusion. A powerful human ruler was ideal. Father offered peace and protection to the creatures of Prescott Woods in exchange for their obedience in constructing Castle Speranza and then Prescott Manor."

Carmen caught a glimpse of her chicken coop's tin roof ahead through the trees. Spare Tire crowed, probably protesting Dax getting too close to his ladies. Carmen emerged alone, blinking, into the bright sunlight. She turned and saw three raccoons waddle from the trees behind her. One with a silver patch of fluffy hair on its head sat back on its haunches and made a shooing gesture towards the house. "All right, all right," she muttered. "I'll make sure the coast is clear."

If Dax had been unsure about the stray cat, he had been downright mistrustful of the three raccoons, especially when they revealed their human visages to him and commenced with chicken relocation. Dax chuffed and complained as he followed at Carmen's heels. Spare Tire allowed Carmen to carry him, although he clucked nonstop and occasionally let out an exasperated crow. Lowell tucked Agatha, the grey Silkie, under one arm and Suellen, the New Hampshire Red, under the other. Brock carried Gretel, Carmen's hefty Jersey Giant, and Korbin reached for black-and-white speckled Bella. Paloma was especially enchanted with Scarlett and Melanie, who backed into a fenced corner of the yard and huddled together, clucking fretfully. She held one fluffy Faverolle in each arm so they could nestle together on the return hike.

* * * *

The walk home was long, arduous and entirely too full of feathers for Carmen's liking. She was fond of Spare Tire, but he gave her a sharp peck or two and she would be relieved to put him down. She wasn't sure what to expect upon arrival to Castle Speranza, only that Brock had assured her that the gnomes and elves would take care of everything.

When she laid eyes upon it at last, Carmen gaped. "It's the most beautiful chicken coop I've ever seen!" she gushed. "Just look at it, Brock!"

Carmen rushed to the new structure, situated behind Castle Speranza between the pond and the woods. An ornate five-foot wrought iron fence surrounded the chicken yard. The fence was gorgeous, but it had nothing on the coop. Like a miniature version of the castle itself, the raised coop was fashioned of interlocking stone. It rested on six short stone columns and even had a tower and a slate roof. Carmen placed Spare Tire on the ground so he could strut around and investigate the new digs. Paloma gently released Scarlett and Melanie. They clung close to Paloma's legs and watched as Gretel, Agatha, Bella, and Suellen raced around the fenced yard and up the ridged ramp into the coop.

"You sure they'll be okay?" Carmen worried. "No trolls will come for a midnight snack?"

"No, the chickens are under our protection now," Brock assured her, "as are you, and the magical beings of the woods will steer clear of them. The friendlier ones, like the tree spirits and elves, will even protect them should the need arise."

"Where are the people who made it?" Carmen wondered. "I'd love to thank them for this."

Brock shrugged. "You don't have to," he answered. "They're just gnomes."

"But this seems awfully permanent, don't you think?" Carmen added. "I mean, as soon as we've stopped the development of the woods and your father has decided he can trust me, I'm going back home and, uh, I want to take my chickens with me."

"Dream on," Paloma muttered. She sat down on the grassy floor of the coop to admire the chickens. "You're not going anywhere. Father would never allow it."

"Nothing is set in stone, Paloma," Brock argued. "Who knows what Father will eventually decide?"

Paloma raised her eyebrows and looked away, clearly unconvinced. Melanie hopped into her lap and snuggled in for some petting.

Korbin and Lowell made their goodbyes. Korbin headed to the library to research chickens and how to maximise egg production. After asking Carmen's permission, Lowell took Dax on a tour of the property. Dax went with the enormous, gruff man happily enough, probably relieved to be away from a noisy, crowing Spare Tire.

Brock took Carmen's hand and led her around to the front of the castle. "Alone at last." He smiled. "Are you doing okay, Carmen?"

"I suppose," she answered, "given that for the foreseeable future I'm staying in a castle built by gnomes surrounded by woods full of magical creatures."

"And with me," Brock amended. "Don't forget that I'll be here." He swept her up into his arms and covered her mouth in a tender kiss.

Carmen's body reacted at once, softening and warming and growing damp in all the right places. She lifted her hand to the back of his neck to stroke his buttery soft skin and urge him to deepen his kiss.

"Hmm," Carmen breathed when Brock's lips parted from hers. His bright blue eyes promised mystery, passion, magic. "This is fascinating and thrilling," she whispered, "and I'm not complaining, Brock, but I hope you understand that I've got to get back home eventually, where I belong. I have friends and a life in Charade."

Brock pressed his lips to hers once more in response. "I'm sure you'd like to freshen up," he told her, "and you must be hungry and thirsty, too."

One and a half seconds later, a waist-high man clad in a roughspun toga stood at Brock's side. He bore a tray holding a goblet of iced liquid and a bunch of plump red grapes in his knobby, oversized hands.

"Ah, refreshments," Brock said. The gnome bobbed his heavily wrinkled head in deference and stood at attention. Carmen accepted the goblet from Brock and took one hesitant sip from it. She licked her lips and downed the glass of sweet, fresh apple juice. Brock took the grapes from the tray and sent the gnome on his way just as Carmen began to thank him for her drink.

"Let me show you the bathing cavern," he said, casting his eyes about as he spoke. "It's where we bathe and, um, restore ourselves."

Carmen noticed a new gravity and nervous uncertainty in his voice. *What could be so ominous about a bathroom?* she wondered.

Brock led her around to the other side of Castle Speranza. Carmen's eyes drank in the peaceful, cool pond when it entered her sight once more. The glassy water reflected the rich blue sky and gnarled tree limbs overhead. Swans glided across the surface, breaking the sharp mirror image into a swirled, blurry impressionist painting. Mama wood duck and her babies were just exiting on the woods' side of the pond. Jewel-toned dragonflies swooped and dove inches over the gleaming surface. Carmen heard the jubilant warble of a wren hidden in the woods.

Chapter Nine

Brock stopped in front of a thick wooden door set into a squat stone structure. The small archway and door were hardly fancy, but looked as though they could stand up to a tornado, an enraged bear, and an earthquake all at once. Brock's gaze flitted from side to side and over his shoulder as he slid the wide wooden bolt. He hurried Carmen inside then shut the door behind him.

Unlike the electrified castle, the tunnel to the bathing cavern was lit only by candles. It felt warm, safe, and almost womb-like to Carmen. She traced her fingertips down the damp, sloping rock wall of the tunnel. At the end of the short walk, the space opened into an enormous cavern. A rushing stream bisected the space, flowing swiftly from right to left, with a swirling, frothy pocket of water and another of bubbling mud. Carmen saw manmade stone enclosures on either side of the entrance.

"Girls' room," he stated and pointed to the right. "Boys' room" — he indicated with a gesture to his left. "The gnomes diverted parts of the stream to use as plumbing down here. There are modern bathrooms in the castle, plumbed by a different stream, but you can use the toilet here as well. I'll meet you at the stream."

Carmen relieved herself in the simple but clean bathroom. It felt odd to have rushing water beneath her, but her urgency helped her get over the discomfiting feeling of a rivulet under her rump.

She found Brock standing nude by the stream's bank and waiting for her. He seemed impatient and nervous. "Come on," he urged. "Strip down and get in here with me. This tub is heated by a natural hot spring. It's amazing."

"All right, all, right." Carmen chuckled. "Where's the fire?" She shucked off her clothes and folded them neatly on the floor of the cavern. Carmen joined Brock next to the bubbling pool, took his hand, and dipped a toe in to test the temperature. "Ooooh! That's boiling!" she complained. "You're gonna poach me!"

"You'll get used to it," Brock insisted. He stepped into the water and sat on a hidden ledge beneath the surface. Carmen eased in beside him. The bubbly current was scorching hot, but soon her body acclimated to it and it felt like pure heaven. The liquid seemed to soak right through her skin and into her bones, lifting away stress and soreness she hadn't even known she'd had. Her breasts floated, buoyant and full, in the steamy eddies. Carmen spread her knees apart so that the currents could tickle the lips of her pussy. She groaned as the water entered her cunt. It felt as thick and soft as a tongue inside her. Carmen spread her legs wider so that the heated bubbles could work their way farther within.

"This feels amazing," she murmured. "I feel drugged. So limp and relaxed, but also so tingly and alive."

"Yes," Brock agreed drowsily. "This bath has some very special qualities." He lolled his head back on the rock edge of the tub and closed his eyes.

Carmen lounged in the natural hot tub for what seemed like hours. She reached a meditative state and time ground to a halt. The water no longer seemed hot—it felt like her exact body temperature. Carmen felt it enter her bloodstream, mingling with her blood and coursing through every vein and artery. It was a living warmth, strengthening her, healing her and changing her somehow. She felt herself rise into the air, light as mist, and coalesce into a cloud, only to plummet downwards in a breathtaking plunge and seep into the ground once more.

Carmen's eyes flew open. "I feel different," she said. "I feel like this water has done something to me."

Under the churning waves, Brock took her hand in his. "Good," he answered. "Now come with me." Carmen let him lead her to the edge of the tub where the hot spring mixed with the underground stream. She gasped when the cold waves lapped over her skin and her sluggishness evaporated. Instead of being unpleasantly chilly, though, the current was invigorating. The stream's depth was just about a foot, so, like Brock, she crawled on her elbows over the smooth river rocks so that she could remain submerged in the brisk, effervescent flow. They moved downstream. Carmen let her legs stretch out behind her and float in the oddly buoyant current. The ripples played against the delicate folds between her legs, replacing the molten heat from the hot tub with refreshing tingles.

Brock paused at the entrance to the mud bath and grinned wickedly. "Ready to get dirty again?" he asked.

"If it's anything like the hot tub, then yeah," she answered. "Definitely."

Brock stepped into the sloppy putty-grey gloop first and held a hand out to steady Carmen as she followed. The mud was hot, although not as hot as the tub they'd just left, and silky-smooth. Carmen moved through the bathwater-warm stuff and found a seat on another hidden ledge next to Brock. Hints of eucalyptus and lavender wafted up from the lapping surface of the bath. "Damn," Carmen noted, "those gnomes were awesome to build this for your family. Did they dig out the whole cavern for you? How did your dad know where to look?" She shifted down on the bench so that the soothing mud was up to her chin.

"The magic folk have used this cavern for centuries," Brock answered, "possibly millennia. It's no accident that Castle Speranza is built right next to this place, you know. Father did have the gnomes enlarge the hot spring and mud baths, and of course they added the bathrooms for us as well."

"Mmmmm," Carmen hummed. She melted into the mud. Her skin, bones, and muscles felt as shapeless and liquid as the sludge in which she sat. Carmen felt herself slip into another meditative state and lost awareness of time and place. Her body dissolved in an ecstasy of release, breaking into living bits of mud, clay and rock, joining with the volatile earth, hardening into stone, disintegrating against the finger-like, curious root of a tree and being drawn into the tree itself, emerging as first flower, then fruit of the tree, before falling back to the soft, welcoming earth and merging once more with the living clay.

Carmen woke to see Brock's face before hers and to feel his splayed hands slip-sliding over her breasts.

She exhaled slowly. "It happened again, like in the hot tub over there," she said, dazzled. "Something changed me. I don't feel the same. What's in this stuff? What's going on?"

"A good thing," Brock replied. He scooted her back against the unseen bench to expose her mud-coated chest. "What's happening now, Carmen," he whispered, "is a very good thing." His hands, greased by the silky gloop, slid over her tits and plucked at her hardened nipples. Carmen closed her eyes and leaned into his caress. Her hair, flecked with brown, stood on end and her lips drew into a sensual pucker.

Brock pressed his spread fingertips into her skin and traced a path up to her neck and over her scalp, then down the back of her head and over her shoulders. Carmen smiled crookedly. "I'm sure I look like a filth monster," she told him, "not to mention the fact that I'm forty years old and no spring chicken, but, God help me, neither of those facts bothers me a bit right now. Brock, you are the hottest man I've ever known. I adore the way you make me feel."

Brock worked his massaging fingers down her back and beneath her ass. "You," he said huskily, "are magnificent, Carmen. Mud is sexy, especially what we've got down here, and I promise you that age means absolutely nothing to me. The way you live, the way you love your town and your friends and your animals, the way you move when you're dancing..."

He knelt in front of her on the floor of the bath and spread her knees. "I want you to enjoy this place," he whispered.

Carmen felt his fingertips nudge the entrance to her cunt. The mud was warm and tingling and slippery — better than any lube on the market — and she arched against his caress as he penetrated her. Heat grew on the stiff tips of her tits and in the sensitive centre of her pussy. Carmen brought one hand to her breast to roll her hardened nipple and lowered the other to Brock's wrist, urging him to fuck her deeper.

Brock's gem-blue eyes darkened. "I find you desirable in every single way, Carmen," he promised her. He lowered his face to hers for a kiss and swirled his tongue in the soft recesses of her mouth.

"Can we do it here?" Carmen whispered. "Will it hurt anything to get this gunk inside me?"

Brock laughed. "Not this gunk," he answered. He turned and lifted her onto her knees on the wide ledge of the bath. "If you want to get fucked, Carmen," he growled, "then by all means you are going to get fucked."

Carmen cried out when he pushed into her. He was inhumanly thick and rock hard, stretching the walls of her pussy until they screamed, but the slick silt eased the friction perfectly.

Carmen curved her back to lift her ass in the air and spread her thighs for him. "Deeper," she begged. Her hanging breasts swept the surface of the mud—it felt like countless tongues lapping at her nipples. "Harder, Brock." She slammed her ass against him and felt the slap-splash of sloppy, wet warmth on her thighs. "Ohhh, God," she gasped. "Whatever you do, don't stop."

"No chance, Carmen," he promised, gripping her hips tightly. "Not until you've come and I've come inside you."

Carmen panted, every inch of skin alive.

"This stuff is good for you, Carmen," he grunted, "because it's now part of you. Do you understand?"

Carmen understood nothing but the tight, hard fucking she was getting. She groaned as her climax bloomed through her body. Her inner muscles gripped his cock in quick, rhythmic spasms that beat inside her like the wings of a trapped bird.

"Oh, yes," she hissed. "It's so good." Just as her own peak began to subside, she felt his cum surge and spurt out of the tip of his cock. The thick, hot mix of semen and silt filled her cunt, as heavy and solid as a fist, and Carmen felt another orgasm build with the rapidity of a rushing train. He held his shaft buried within her until her whimpers quieted.

Brock sat beside her on the ledge of the bath. Carmen, muscles shaking, took a deep breath. "Fuck, that was good, Brock," she told him and gave her dirt-spiked head a shake. "I've never come close to having sex that amazing."

"Although I'd like to," Brock said, "I can't take all the credit. A lot of the heightened sensitivity you're feeling is a result of the unique properties down here."

"Hmm," Carmen hummed. She leant back into the soothing, warm gloop and turned his words over in her mind. "You said this stuff is now part of me," she recalled. "What exactly did you mean, Brock?"

"I mean that life as you know it is over," he answered, "and a new life has begun."

Carmen laughed uneasily. "Uh, look, Brock, the sex was pretty amazing, but I wouldn't say you're ruined other guys for me for the rest of my life."

Brock stood up, looking like a living terracotta statue of the perfect male, then eased into the cool flow of the stream. The silt billowed from his skin in a dirt-brown cloud and disappeared with the rushing current. He tipped his head back in the water and scrubbed the earth from his scalp, then sat upright and shook his head like a dog. Carmen, grinning, raised one hand to shield herself from the watery spray. Brock ruffled his fingers through his ashy-grey hair to stand it on end and beckoned to Carmen. "Care to join me for a rinse, my filthy princess?" he asked.

Carmen sighed and rubbed her thighs together beneath the surface of the gloopy stuff. Her questions and worries melted away, overshadowed completely by sensory pleasure. "Mmmmm, I'm not ready to get out," she protested. "It just feels so good in here, Brock." Brock's eyes darkened with interest as she lifted her hands to her breasts and slid her fingers over her muddied skin. Experimentally, she shoved her tits together so that they made a squelching sound then released them to create slow ripples. "Are you sure it's time to get clean, Brock?" Brock watched her hand disappear into the liquid earth. Carmen lifted her feet up to the bench on either side of her and sat, splayed like a frog, with her knees above the surface of the bath. "I wish I could tell you how good this feels," she whispered. A soft smile played on her lips as she found the slickened entrance to her pussy with her hand.

Brock swallowed. He stole a glance towards the entrance of the bathing cavern. The smooth stone archway flickered in the warm torchlight. "Believe me when I say that I'd love nothing more than to join you," he admitted, "but we should really be getting out of here. It's not entirely, uh, appropriate…"

Carmen's mouth fell open as her fingers pushed their way between her legs. "It's like this stuff is making everything more sensitive somehow," she murmured, oblivious to his concerns. "Every bit of my skin seems more alive now, as though there were extra nerves and blood in it." She found her swollen G-spot with one fingertip. "Oh, God," she groaned, "even the bumps of my knuckles going into my cunt feels like heaven." Carmen slowly ground her hips against her hand, creating gentle, sloppy waves. Beneath the surface of the crystal-clear stream, she saw Brock's penis stiffen once more.

"Fuck it," he grunted, and heaved his body back into the mudbath with a plopping splash.

Brock covered Carmen's mouth with his and thrust his tongue inside. He settled between her raised knees and pulled her hand away. "My turn," he said roughly and pressed his erection between her legs.

Carmen slid her hand between the clenching cheeks of his rump and found his tight hole with one fingertip. He pushed his shaft, already thick and engorged, into her cunt as she eased her finger in and out of his ass. "Nice?" she whispered.

The pupils of Brock's eyes were so dilated that only the faintest ring of blue was visible. He grunted in agreement and kissed her again, keeping his shaft buried in the warm embrace of her pussy. His kiss was deliciously sweet and wet, a perfect mix of yielding and strong.

"Aw, fuck," Carmen murmured into his mouth. "What are you doing to me, Brock?"

"My question exactly," an angry female voice answered. "What the *fuck* are you doing to her, Brock?"

Chapter Ten

Carmen's eyes flew open. For a split-second, they met Brock's. She saw surprise, irritation, and, oddly, fear flash through them before he slid out of her and sat beside her on the submerged seat. He glared silently at Paloma as Gavin, Korbin and Lowell joined her.

"I'd ask you to explain yourself," Gavin snarled, "except that it's entirely obvious what's happening here. You have taken it upon yourself to break the most important rule I have established for our family. No one—*no one*—is to come to the bathing cavern except for others of the wood."

"I knew exactly what you'd say, Father," Brock charged back at him, "and I knew that you'd be wrong. Prescott Wood is in real danger. We need Carmen. It's not fair to ask her to help us and to place herself in harm's way if we don't let her bathe in the Healing Waters and the Living Earth."

"Oh, right," Paloma scoffed. "You're all about what's fair and honourable, Brock. This has nothing to do with the fact that you just want to have her around as your permanent playmate, does it?"

Carmen cleared her throat uneasily. "Look, guys, I'm really sorry that I've offended you by being down here. I had no idea it would upset you so much." She shot Brock an irritated glance and continued. "I'll leave now, and I won't come back, and I won't ever tell anyone about it, okay? And I'm still happy to help you keep Prescott Wood from being developed."

The expressions on Brock's family's faces grew even more grim.

"I'm afraid it's not so simple," Korbin said quietly. "Now that you've been here, now that you've bathed in the water and the mud..." He shrugged and looked away. "Now, like us, you are immortal. You have certain gifts and strengths, true, but you must also remain close by. We must bathe in the water and mud once every day, or else our lives come to a rapid and painful end."

Carmen spun on Brock, spitting venom. "Are you telling me that you changed me—changed my *life*—without even discussing it with me? Don't you think I ought to have been involved in the decision, Brock?"

"What in the hell were you thinking?" Lowell thundered. "It's not up to you, Brock. This is our stronghold, our safe place, and no mortals may ever enter it. Father has kept us safe and set apart for over two hundred years."

"Ah, it's all starting to make sense now," Carmen seethed. She pointed an accusing finger at Brock, whose feathery, ash-grey hair stood wildly on end. "You came to these woods when you were just seven years old, Brock. Sure, you've lived for over two hundred years, and, what's that you said? Age means nothing to you?" She laughed mercilessly. "Age means nothing to you because you are still a *child*, Brock. You want what you want, and fuck your family and fuck me if we happen to want something different. You believe you know best and you don't give a shit what anyone else feels."

Gavin raised one hand and silence fell in the candlelit cavern. His face was as cold and stony as the rock walls above the rushing underground stream. "No one can say that I do not love my children," Gavin said calmly. "I have hewn a home for them in these woods and devoted myself to their safety. Brock, you have violated the trust I have placed in you. By bringing this woman to our home and then permitting her to bathe in this place, you have forever broken the bond between us."

The colour drained from Brock's caramel-brown skin until he looked as pale as a glass of skim milk.

"You are banished, Brock. You are no longer welcome in my home or in these bathing caverns. Be gone."

Brock's jaw worked and cords of strained tendons stood out on his mud-spattered neck. "It's a mistake, Father," he argued. "You need me to save the woods, and you need Carmen, too."

Gavin took one menacing step towards the mudbath. "Get out," he ordered.

Slowly, Brock rose. Carmen caught a glimpse of his finely sculpted body, slickened with mud, before he splashed into the underground stream. Briskly, he scrubbed the silt from his nude body and climbed out on the rock bank of the stream. Korbin handed him a pair of rough grey wool trousers, a long-sleeved thermal shirt, and a pair of brown leather boots. After dressing hurriedly, Brock paused to look at his siblings and father.

"Goodbye, then, family. I wish it hadn't come to this." Only Korbin looked sympathetic. Paloma, Lowell and Gavin stared coldly back at him. "And good luck, Carmen. I never meant to hurt or offend you. I just believed that it would be easier to make you one of us first and explain it all later." He chuckled sadly. "Maybe I am just a child, after all."

He took a deep breath and exited the cavern.

Carmen, still soaking in the warm mud bath and seething about Brock's actions, waited for one of the others to speak. The silence seemed to amplify until it became unbearable. "So, what now?" she asked at last.

Gavin shook his head. "You cannot leave, that's for certain. Not now. Your future is tied forever to Fair Woods and to the Living Waters. To live elsewhere would mean death. True, you are new to magic and young in mortal years. You do not require a daily visit to the waters as we do now, but you must still bathe here every few days, or else your life will ebb from you as the traces of Healing Waters and Living Earth fade away. We will teach you our ways and make a home for you here. We will feed you and clothe you and teach you our ways." He gritted his teeth. "Perhaps one day you will even learn to like it here. Regardless, you must stay. Brock has made that decision for you and for all of us." He turned and began to walk towards the cavern's exit.

"Wait a minute, Gavin," Carmen called out. "If living elsewhere means death for me, then doesn't it mean the same thing for Brock?"

Gavin's stony gaze remained fixed on the exit tunnel. His broad shoulders lifted and fell with a ragged breath.

"Like, I understand that he's a pain in the ass, but he is your son, after all. Did you just sentence your own son to death, Gavin?"

"You understand nothing, woman," Gavin retorted. He wheeled about and bellowed at her, "Time and time again, Brock has endangered all that I've worked so hard to build here. He ventures into Charade to observe humans, including you, I suppose, for his own amusement, and has come close to revealing our secrets on numerous occasions. He pushes the boundaries of where he may safely travel and still visit the Healing Waters and the Living Earth on a daily basis. He pesters me for greater contact with the mortal world. He doesn't understand that out there is only pain, loss, disease and death." He threw her own words back at her. "As you said, Brock is a child. He is a child who endangers the rest of our lives and I will no longer tolerate his presence."

Carmen rose, clothed only in a thin layer of shining brown silt. "You know what I think, Gavin?" she challenged him, dripping, with her hands on her hips. "I think you're a real asshole."

Gavin's eyes narrowed dangerously.

"I think you were devastated when your wife died, and I'm sorry for that, but dude—it was two hundred years ago! You've locked your kids away so that the only company they have is elves and gnomes and trees and maybe a squirrel or two. How are they supposed to grow up when you hide them away from the world? You don't have to date, although, frankly, you seem like one guy who could do with a good pleasure-fuck if I've ever seen one. What you *do* have to do is give your kids, who are now over two centuries old, by the way, a little more freedom and access to the world."

Carmen stared down the massive patriarch of the family.

Gavin scowled back at her. "You may not tell me what I must and must not do, woman," he growled. "Since you are so eager to defend Brock, you may follow him into the woods. You've sealed your own fate with your rash words. I've no doubt you'll live to regret them when you're wandering far from this place and your life is slipping away. I have been told that the pain is excruciating."

"The fact that you would send your own son to die in such a manner shows your true character, Gavin," Carmen said, "and, in case you missed it before, you're a real asshole." She walked to the edge of the stream and jumped in. After hurriedly rinsing the dirt from her hair, face and body, Carmen emerged and dressed herself in her discarded clothes. She felt the others' eyes on her as she yanked her jeans up over her damp skin, but was too furious and disgusted to care.

"You guys can stay here if you like," she directed at Korbin, Lowell and Paloma, "but I'm going to go try to save your brother. He may be a self-centred child, but he doesn't deserve to die alone in the woods."

Carmen dashed from the flickering cavern into the darkness of nightfall. She heard Gavin's enraged bellow follow her, "Best save yourself while you're at it, woman!"

Moonlight glimmered on the calm surface of the pond. Carmen stood and listened. She heard the muffled padding steps of an opossum, the soft rustle of a corn snake, and the dive-and-snatch of an owl on the hunt. She caught traces of thistle and honeysuckle in the air, and felt the cool, moist air brush against her cheek. Her senses seemed more powerful than before — they flooded her with sensory input, but Carmen had no time to think about that. She needed to find Brock and find some way to get him back to the Healing Waters and the Living Earth before it was too late.

Carmen squinted and scanned the ground for signs of Brock's path, but found no hint about the course he'd taken. "Brock! Brock, where are you?" she yelled. A coyote's shrill howl answered her.

"Great," Carmen muttered. "Just great. All I need to do is search the entirety of Fair Woods completely by myself to find a bratty two-hundred-year-old before he dries up and — dies." She felt a furry bump under her palm and looked down. Dax gazed up at her with a loyal, concerned expression. "Okay, then," Carmen said. "Not entirely by myself, at any rate. Come on, good boy."

Dax chuffed and followed Carmen into the blackness of Prescott Woods.

* * * *

Four hours later, Carmen felt ready to cry. Her bare feet — *why* hadn't she thought to grab her shoes when she'd stormed from the cavern? — were sore and bloodied from innumerable scratches. Her voice was a raspy caw from hours of yelling in vain for Brock. She was exhausted, thirsty, frantic and utterly at a loss about what to do. Dax whined beside her. He seemed to sense the urgency of the situation.

Carmen's gaze fell on an enormous live oak tree. Its wide branches spread far overhead and mingled into the foliage around her. At its base, the roots created an inviting hollow that was filled with dry leaves. Just looking at the cosy nook made a yawn sneak out of

Carmen's throat. Dax, her canine enabler, left her side and planted himself on the ground next to the tree. He cocked his head at her as if in invitation.

"All right," Carmen gave in. "Just for a few minutes, just to gather my strength." She nestled into the pile of leaves and leant back against the tree's furrowed bark. It felt like the most divinely feather-plumped, silk-upholstered bedding imaginable. Dax settled against her and placed his heavy head on her thigh. Carmen fell into a deep, delicious sleep.

Chapter Eleven

Hours later, sunlight filtered through the treetops and fell on her closed eyelids. Carmen adjusted her shoulders' position on the wide trunk of the tree and drowsily stroked Dax's golden fur. Her brow creased slightly as she considered the pros and cons of gaining consciousness. Something stirred importantly under the heavy blanket of sleep — something troubling and time-sensitive. A life-or-death matter...

"Brock!" Carmen shouted. Distraught, she sat up and looked about. Dax jumped to his paws and barked with concern. Carmen raced into the woods and resumed her search. Dax, ever loyal, matched her step-for-step throughout the long day. Carmen caught fleeting glimpses of curious, inhuman faces in the shadows as she searched, but she had only one face on her mind. "He may be a self-centred brat," Carmen muttered, "but he doesn't deserve this." She paused only to relieve herself, munch a few apples from an opportune tree and drink fresh water from an overland stream. However, as the sun began to go down, Carmen had still seen neither hide nor hair of

Brock. She cupped her hands around her mouth and yelled at the top of her lungs, "Brock! Brock!"

A shrill sound erupted at Carmen's back. Just two feet away, a minuscule person laughed uproariously. Carmen's eyes widened when she saw the misshapen creature. Beneath a tattered leather dress, wide hips and the faint curve of a bosom revealed that the strange being was female. A long beak of a nose curled down over a pair of thin lips, and a sharp chin jutted out above a skinny neck. Through the dirt-brown snarls of hair, Carmen saw that the ears — though both enormous — were shaped entirely differently. One was long, with a flabby, pendulous earlobe, and one was squashed and plump like a cauliflower. Like the gnome who'd brought refreshments on the lawn of Castle Speranza, this creature's hands were twisted and knobby at the end of scrawny wrists. A wide stripe of fur rose on Dax's back and he took one step backwards.

"She dersen't worry about the poochie," the gnome squeaked in a high voice. "Poochie sees but a wee skunk, that he does!" She giggled so hard that she snorted. "Poor poochie dersen't know why a skunk can speak like his mistress, though! Poor poochie!"

"Poor poochie, indeed," Carmen muttered, and resumed her desperate cries. "Brock? Can you hear me?" she screamed. "Where are you?"

"She's looking for someone, then? Someone in need of her help, yes! Poor somebody, all alone and groany-moaning in the woods!" The gnome fell on her back and rolled from side to side, clutching her stomach in mockery.

"You've seen him?" Carmen asked. "Where? Take me to him!"

The gnome rolled her eyes and writhed in faux-pain, then burst into laughter at her own joke.

Carmen squatted beside her. "Take me to him, please!"

"Aye, then." The gnome quieted. She fixed a bright, clever eye on Carmen. "She's new to the magic, and new to the ways of the wood, so perhaps she's not knowing the way of things. The people of the fine castle order us about, yes, and lord over the wood, yes, but perhaps they dersen't say the thank yous that they might be saying. They dersen't show kindness to the older folk of the wood." She knelt and pointed one gnarled finger at Carmen's chest. "Perhaps she can make the fine castle folk be kinder to the old folk of the wood, yes?"

"Oh, ah," Carmen stuttered. With effort, she kept her expression steady, although the blast of foul breath from the gnome's mouth was horrendous. "I—I can certainly try. It's just... I haven't known them for long. I don't know exactly what I can do to help you and I'm not at all sure I can make them listen to me, anyway."

The gnome woman raised her shaggy eyebrows and stood. "Ah, well. More's the pity for her, and pity-more-the-greater for yon feller in the wood, growing wrinklier and sicklier by the minute. She can do nothing to help? Well, aye, then, neither can I." The gnome skipped around the back of the great live oak tree as the last rays of sunlight faded from the woods and were replaced by the glow of a bright, full moon.

"Wait!" Carmen shouted. "I can help! I will help, I promise!"

The gnome leaned around the tree trunk and assessed Carmen. "She promises?"

Carmen nodded with enthusiasm.

"She promises that the fine castle folk will invite us to use their bathing place, since it was first ours anyways?"

Carmen agreed.

"She promises that the fine castle folk will speak to us gently, by our names, and never more a rough hand laid on us?" The gnome leant forwards and raised one horny-nailed finger. "She promises that the fine castle folk will give us some of them fine chicken eggies we've been smelling?"

Carmen bit her lip to keep from smiling — who'd have guessed what lifesavers Scarlett, Suellen and the rest of the flock had turned out to be? — and agreed wholeheartedly.

"She understands that breaking her promise to me means an end to her? A very ugly, bad business of an end, too, that I'd not wish on the foulest troll." The gnome shuddered.

"Yes, yes, I promise!" Carmen said.

"She comes, then," the gnome whispered. She darted away into the woods. Carmen, with Dax at her heels, scrambled to chase her through the dark, dense growth of trees.

* * * *

Twenty minutes later the gnome stopped and pointed down into a shallow ravine. "Yonder he rests," she whispered.

Carmen's heart fell when she saw the withered, thin form of a man on the ground. His hollowed chest rose and fell unevenly. She worked her way down into the vine-covered ravine and took his hand delicately.

"Brock?" she whispered. "Is that you?" The man looked like a corpse. His thin skin draped over his bones like wet tissue paper so that the contours of his skull stood in sharp relief. Wisps of white hair dotted his bare scalp, and the knobby ball of his Adam's apple worked in his throat.

The man's lips moved, but no sound came from his mouth. He licked his lips with a pale, gummy tongue and tried again. "Carmen," he rasped. "Too late. So sorry." A wet gurgle rose from his throat.

"Ach, he's in a bad place, this one." The gnome tsk-tsked at Carmen's shoulder. "He's needing those Healing Waters and that Living Earth, yes, indeed."

Carmen's eyes stung. She turned to the gnome and begged, "Is there anything you can do?"

"Ah, then, she needs more help from us?" the gnome sighed. "She knows she can't get this one to the spring at the fine castle, and she wants us to show her where we old folk of the wood find the Healing Waters and the Living Earth, does she?"

Carmen fought the urge to throttle the gnome and forced a gentle smile on her face. "Yes, please," she answered. "Please show me where you use the Healing Waters and the Living Earth."

The gnome woman gave a melodramatic sigh. "She wants us to believe that she will be kind to we old ones of the wood, and she hasn't even asked our name! How can she properly say thank you to us when she doesn't know our name?"

Brock stared silently upward through milky eyes as his breath rattled in his chest.

Carmen felt that she would chomp her tongue in two if she bit it any harder. "I am so sorry," she said. "How rude of me to skip our introduction. My name is Carmen. What is your name?"

The gnome beamed with delight and exposed all six of her long, yellowed teeth. "I'm Mephita," she said with pride. "It means 'skunk'."

"What a lovely name," Carmen answered, thinking that it was perfectly fitting as well. She suppressed a wince of disgust as Mephita exhaled another noxious puff of breath.

"Come on, then, you," ordered Mephita. "Bring on that bag of bones feller before he turns into dust. No time to waste."

Carmen lifted Brock's limp body, which now weighed less than Dax's. It was shocking and heartbreaking, but she was grateful that she was easily able to carry him and trail Mephita. Brock moaned in her arms as she followed Mephita down to the bottom of the ravine. Like wind-blown dandelion puffs, the last white wisps of hair floated away from his head and left his bald scalp bare and vulnerable.

Mephita disappeared around a bend. Carmen hurried to catch her. She jostled Brock with her jogging steps and murmured apologies when he cringed in pain. Carmen found Mephita standing over three loaf-sized rocks placed in the shape of a triangle. The gnome looked like a strange statue herself, outlined in the moon's glow. Mephita knelt and leaned over the rocks with her eyes closed. She murmured guttural, indecipherable words and bent to kiss the ground in the middle of the triangle.

At once, a sparkling fountain of water bubbled up from the centre of the three rocks. At each corner, where the three rocks met, wet mud oozed from the ground and spread slowly onto the dry earth.

Mephita rocked back on her heels and smiled in triumph. "There you have it, Carmen. Healing Water and Living Earth. It's only good for a few minutes, so best get the feller into it right away. He's near the end, that one."

Carmen settled Brock on the ground next to the fountain and placed his head on one side of the rock-formation. His gaunt skull was held in place by the ropy tendons of his throat, and his opaque eyes continued to stare senselessly up into the tree branches. He no longer looked like he was about to die — he looked like a man who'd been dead for days and days.

Carmen collected some of the icy-cold water in her hands and dribbled it into Brock's mouth. His chin moved slightly and the liquid gushed down his neck. "Swallow it, Brock," Carmen urged. She daubed mud onto his withered hands and forearms. The cool drink seemed to revive him a bit, she thought, but he still looked like he had passed death's doorway and was hanging his coat in death's foyer. Carmen poured more water between his lips and wept with relief to see him take a deep swallow. She opened his shirt and plastered Living Earth onto the stark cave of his ribcage and over the scrawny pipe of his throat. Colour slowly began to return to his pale, papery skin.

Carmen pulled his shoes off and ladled handfuls of Healing Water onto his bony feet, and revisited the bared skin on his chest with fresh applications of wet earth. Brock still looked like a corpse, but at least now he looked like a freshly-deceased one.

"Thank you," he rasped. "Thank you, Carmen. I was going to die out here."

"You don't need to thank me," Carmen answered, busily splashing and rubbing his hands and chest. "I'm still pissed at you," she admitted, "but you don't deserve to be cast out by your own family to die all alone." She scooped a double-handful of gloppy soil on his bare scalp and applied it to his head.

Brock swallowed and managed a weak grin. "So what do you think of the aged version of me, Carmen? I'm not quite someone you'd invite into your bed right now, am I?"

Carmen cupped water and worked it into the silty crust on his chest, which was beginning to fill out with musculature and regain a tan colour. She placed one damp palm on his sunken cheek. "You forget what I am now," she said. A smile played at the corner of her mouth. "I'm now one of the Fair Folk, am I not? Age means nothing to me."

Brock chuckled. "Indeed you are, Carmen."

Thin grey hair spouted over his scalp through a chalky layer of drying mud. Fascinated, Carmen anointed him with another handful of the precious liquid that bubbled from between the rocks. The ash-grey hair grew and thickened before her eyes like a time lapse video of grass growing from seed.

Unsteadily, Brock rose to a sitting position next to the gurgling font. He lowered his face to the six-inch fountain and drank deeply, then turned to Carmen with a mischievous glimmer in his sapphire eyes. "Perhaps it's not so bad," he asked softly. "Immortality, enhanced senses, the ability to cast glamours...and close proximity to yours truly?" He rubbed more dampened silt over his cheeks and over the darkening skin of his chest.

"Perhaps not," Carmen admitted, "but don't forget the close proximity to your family, either." Brock bent to take another drink. His hands had lost their skeletal appearance and his shoulders now looked more substantial. "The point is, Brock, that you didn't ask me first," she went on. "You don't get to just make choices about my life for me, especially choices that are irreversible. I have friends, jobs, a house and a community that I love. If I have to say goodbye to them, I want to be the one to do it, even if I get to have immortality and super-senses and glamours."

Brock took one of her hands in his. "And me," he added. "You get to have me, too, Carmen." Goosebumps prickled down Carmen's arms as Brock pressed his lips to her fingertips. "I'm not so bad, am I?" He traced the tip of his tongue over her palm, and Carmen shuddered with want. She threw a glance back at Mephita, who watched the exchange with a lewd expression, and yanked her hand away.

"The point, Brock," she insisted, "is that you didn't *ask* me for my thoughts. This goes way beyond picking me up for a surprise weekend holiday without running it by me beforehand, and even that would bug me a little bit. You can't just change my life because you think it's best. I have to choose it."

Brock held his hands in the bubbling fountain and studied her face as though he were seeing it for the first time. All traces of his mirth were gone.

"Yes, I think you're hot," Carmen told him, "and yes, immortality is cool, but I can't have any kind of future with a self-centred pleasure-seeker who makes my choices for me. I've lived for forty years, Brock, and I've learnt that I'm only happy if I can be in charge of my own destiny. After two hundred years of being a kid prince of the woods, I don't think it's even possible for you to grow up."

Brock's bearing visibly cooled, even as his body regained its usual heated virility. He knelt and gulped deep mouthfuls of Healing Water from the spring then washed the traces of Living Earth from his face, scalp, chest and arms. He stood. "You should have something to drink, too, Carmen," he told her. "Just to be on the safe side."

Carmen knelt and drank from the fountain, which was now noticeably shorter in height. The liquid had a sweet, faintly lemony taste. She felt it move down her throat to her stomach, where it seemed to radiate energy throughout her entire body. She took another swallow. Energy from the water sent shivers down her spine that pooled between her legs.

She rocked back on her heels and wiped her mouth with the back of her hand. Brock looked good enough to eat. His skin glowed a rich caramel colour and his silky ash-grey hair once more stood lushly on end. Her eyes made their way down his wet shirt, now plastered over his rippled abdomen, and over the unmistakable bulge in his trousers. Carmen's cunt melted in luxurious anticipation. She knew that nothing would be more delicious than to send Mephita on her way, open up the fly of Brock's pants, and take that thick cock between her lips. She salivated, remembering the sweet, rich tang of his cum in her mouth.

But no, she thought. *Perhaps his choices brought me to this place, but I'm going to assert myself. Otherwise I'll end up under his control, just as he and his siblings are bossed around by Gavin. Fuck that,* she decided. She heard a sputter from the fountain and saw that it was only barely visible above ground. The flow of oozing silt from between the rocks had stopped and begun to crackle and dry. *If I'm going to live forever in these woods, I'm going to make my own choices and control my own destiny.* The fountain's flow stopped and the last of the Healing Water seeped into the ground. *Or die trying.*

Mephita bounced on the balls of her feet. "All better then?" she chirped.

"Beat it, gnome," he mumbled. "Carmen and I have things to do. We'll call you if we need you again, so listen close."

"O-ho, you! I think not!" Mephita retorted. "This one, Carmen, made a promise to me on pain of death. You and the fine folk of your castle will be treating the gnomes different now, feller." Mephita stood and braced her gnarled hands on her bony hips. "That's me, and my kin, and all the old ones in the wood."

Brock scowled and looked to Carmen for explanation.

"It's really not fair for your family to be rude to them," she told him. "Mephita wants you to allow the gnomes to bathe at the bathing cavern near the castle, and she wants you to address them by name, with no physical roughness, and to say please and thank you when they work."

Brock ran one hand through his hair and nodded. "Okay, okay," he agreed. "I suppose that's only fair. Anything else?"

Mephita leant forwards. "Eggsies!" she hissed. "Don't be forgetting the eggsies, Carmen!"

"You promised her chicken eggs?" Brock asked. "Seriously?"

"What's the problem?" Carmen asked. "The girls are good layers! Although," she conceded, "I may need to let the flock increase a little bit to keep up with egg demand."

Mephita chortled with glee.

"Right, then." Brock nodded. "Thank you, Mephita, for your help in saving me. I really appreciate it. Please call me Brock."

"You're welcome, Brock!" hooted Mephita.

Brock winced and leaned away from the gnome. "The way I see it, Carmen and Mephita," he continued, "is that we need to save the woods immediately, both in order to keep the peace and to restore our place at Castle Speranza."

Carmen nodded and gestured for him to go on. Mephita sat on a rock and listened intently, her bulbous head cocked to one side.

"We need to convince Old Man Prescott that selling the land is a bad idea. If we can't remind him of his family's obligation to protect the woods, then we need to make him believe it's a bad idea for some other reason. Otherwise, we'll end up relying on Mephita here for our Healing Waters and our Living Mud, and my family will resort to violence."

Mephita tapped one thickened, yellow fingernail on her chin. "You and you should take me along," she leaned in front of Brock's face and stated matter-of-factly. "You dersen't want to risk another day with none of the Healing Waters for yourself, then, do you, Brock?" Brock's nostrils flared. He squinted and nodded in agreement.

"Yes, Mephita, we would appreciate your help very much. Summoning the Healing Waters and the Living Earth from the earth are skills that I lack, and they are skills that we need very much right now. I would be grateful if you accompanied us to Prescott Manor."

Mephita scampered over the crest of the ridge. "Best we're going, then!" she urged. "Best we go!"

Chapter Twelve

Carmen and Brock worked their way up the loose ground of the ravine and began the long hike towards Prescott Manor with Mephita. Along the way, they found a ring of earthy-sweet mushrooms and a tree with tart pears, but Carmen's stomach protested noisily nonetheless by the time they reached the edge of the woods. Mephita summoned another gush of Healing Waters so that they could refresh themselves, then they scoped out Prescott Manor.

Across an expanse of lawn, the great home rose in Georgian grandeur. After hearing about the secluded property for years, Carmen was both pleased and disappointed to see it at last. She was surprised to note that the building itself was the only grand thing about the estate. The lawn was dry and bare in places, the three-tiered fountain was dry, and weeds blended with the landscape around the structure such that it was one unruly mass of greenery. Even under the moon's soft light, the place was a dump.

"Does he still live here?" Carmen wondered aloud. "The place is so run-down!"

"Oh, yes, he's here all right," Brock said through gritted teeth. "I see the old traitor through the upstairs window." Brock pointed to a yellow square of light on the second floor. A man's form stood at the window facing the woods then moved away out of sight.

Brock's hand tightened into a fist. "Damn Prescott and his greed," he muttered. "Doesn't he know that everything he has is thanks to us?"

Carmen placed one cool hand on his shoulder. "Remember, Brock, we're going to do this your way, with no violence. You're not your father or Gavin, both of whom are ready to tear apart anything that opposes them. You're not your bloodthirsty sister, who's daydreaming about switchblades. You're also not Korbin, who's content to let others deal with the problem and hope for the best." She gave his thick shoulder a squeeze. "We can fix this without harming a hair on Old Man Prescott's head."

Inside, Calvin Prescott eased his bare feet into worn slippers. The manor, with its stone walls and marble floors, was cool even in the summer, but with electricity costs the way they were, using the heater was a luxury reserved for the coldest days of winter. As he shut his bedroom door, a puff of dust blew down from one of the few paintings left in the place. Calvin sneezed mightily and made his way downstairs.

He leaned against the counter as he waited for the kettle to boil and daydreamed. *Once I finalise the sale,* he thought lazily, *I'll call in some of those people who buy antiques and such and clear out the rest of this place. Then I'll put the manor on the market. Even in its current condition, it's a fine home.* His eyes watered and he scrubbed at them with the back of his hand then continued his mental planning. *I'll pocket the earnings and deposit them and head south. I'll find a nice place near the ocean where it's always warm. The Florida Keys, perhaps?*

The kettle began to scream and Calvin removed it from the stove. After pouring the steaming water into his teapot to seep, he placed it on a tray with a teacup and a plate of sardines and crackers and walked into his library. There he eased into a threadbare armchair, snapped on the floor lamp next to him, and opened a leather-bound book. J.M. Barrie's 'Peter Pan', the story of a magical world in which children never grow up, might have been written for kids, but it was Calvin's favourite literary indulgence.

The manor creaked and moaned as it settled in for the evening. Calvin didn't flinch when the faint pop-and-slide of an opening window issued from a nearby room. "All alone in an old house once more," he mumbled, "like so many nights before." He assembled a sardine on a cracker and took a thoughtful bite. "But not," he added, "for very much longer."

Calvin took a sip of his tea and picked up his book. He let one hand dangle over the arm of his chair as he read about a strange shadow in the Darlings' London home. It took several moments before he realised that a soft furriness grazed against his fingertips. "Huh?" he muttered. "A cat? I don't have a cat."

He looked down at the floor and his eyes widened. Glossy black fur, long white stripes, thick bushy tail — *skunk!* Calvin scrambled over the opposite arm of the chair and lurched towards the door. The animal walked towards him slowly, making bird-like squeaks, and waved its tail.

"Sh-sh-sh-shhh," Calvin whispered. "Good little skunkie! Everything's just fine." The skunk trotted towards him. Calvin made his way to the back door, keeping one eye out for furniture impediments and one eye fixed on the creature before him. He reached the back door and paused with one hand on the knob. The skunk turned its rump towards him and gracefully raised its back legs.

Calvin's scream filled the empty house and spilled over into the neglected lawn. He fell through the back door onto his ass and crab-walked away from the house in terror. The skunk followed him out of the door and chased him across the lawn.

Calvin was running backwards for dear life when he tripped over a prone body and fell to the ground.

"Now just look at what you've done!" a woman shrieked. "Are you trying to kill this poor man?" Beside the woman, a yellow Lab whimpered.

"The skunk! There's a skunk!" Calvin protested. He held a shaking hand up and pointed back towards the manor. A black and white tuxedo cat sat where he'd indicated. It lifted one paw and licked it with a casual air.

"Don't get out much, do you?" the woman snorted. "Where I'm from, we call that a cat."

Calvin shook his head in bafflement.

"Anyhoodle, I'm Margie McCrory, and this is my associate, David Donaldson." The woman held out one hand and Calvin shook it in a daze. Her eyes were magnified behind coke-bottle glasses and her salt-and-pepper hair was pulled into a face-stretching bun. "David twisted his ankle in the woods back there" — she indicated Prescott Woods with a jerk of her chin — "and I'm afraid he's going to need some medical attention. I hope you've got good insurance." She snorted.

"Excuse me, but I'm Calvin Prescott, and this is my property. The woods and the manor are clearly marked 'No Trespassing.' Please explain your presence here before I call the police." Calvin stood and brushed off his threadbare shirt.

"Well, Mr Prescott, you should know us, then." Margie chortled. "We work for the Morgan Group. They hired us to do a geological survey of the woods before the purchase is finalised."

"Ah," Calvin said. "It was my understanding that the inspection process was complete. There was an inspection done last month, was there not?"

"Well, yes," Margie agreed, "and that's why we're here. Turns out the inspection raised some red flags upon further, ah, inspection. The Morgan Group wanted us to dig a little deeper."

Sprawled on the dry grass before them, David Donaldson groaned in pain. "My ankle..." he complained. David's face was deeply lined and speckled with brown age-spots. He raised one sinewy hand to his sparse ash-grey hair.

"Poor David." Margie shook her head. "We were checking out some of your sinkholes and his foot fell right through. I had a devil of a time pulling him free and out here to your lawn. It appears to be broken. Frankly, I'm astonished that you attempted to have this land developed, Mr Prescott, what with the sinkholes."

"What?" Calvin sputtered.

"Don't forget the grey bat," David moaned.

"And the grey bat. It's endangered, of course, and Prescott Woods is one of its few remaining habitats.

"Grey bat?" Calvin shot back. "How on earth am I supposed to know about the grey bat?"

The cat hissed at Calvin and began to groom its back with long licks.

Margie cleared her throat and withdrew a binder from her backpack. "I see here, Mr Prescott, that you vouched that you had no knowledge of any land malformations in your woods that would hinder development. You stated that you had perused the entirety of the woods during your teenage years and that it was stable and pristine. 'Ideal for a housing development,' you said here." Margie thrust a paper at him and pointed to his signature. "Mr Prescott, the sinkholes in the woods are hundreds of years old. The land surface of the woods is a thin crust atop a network of limestone caves. Had you, in fact, perused these woods in their entirety, you would have learnt that fact rather quickly."

"I have no recollection of signing that document," Calvin argued, "and I've never seen or heard of any sinkholes. I'm going to call Marvin Morgan right now to get to the bottom of this. He should have let me know you were coming to inspect." Calvin's eyes narrowed suspiciously.

"What about the grey bat?" insisted David. "You can't just wipe out the grey bat, Mr Prescott! It's endangered!"

Calvin jabbed his finger alternately at David and Margie. "I don't give two shits about the grey bat," he fumed. "As far as I'm concerned, there could be unicorns and albino flying monkeys in those woods. I'm selling it and packing my bags. I'm tired of living in this rickety old place by myself, and I'm sick of seclusion for the sake of some old family custom. If you're genuinely from the Morgan Group, then submit your findings. Otherwise, get off of my property before the cops arrive. Forget Marvin Morgan—I'm calling the police immediately."

The cat paused its bathing with one hind foot in the air and yowled.

Calvin began to march back to Prescott Manor. "Mr Prescott, houses built in the woods will crumble and people will be hurt, and it'll all come back to haunt you!" Margie shouted after him. "You're going to regret this!"

Without turning, Calvin waved them away with one hand and kept walking. Margie's and David's visages were replaced by those of Carmen and Brock. "What the hell are we going to do?" Carmen whispered.

"Cal, baby, is that you?" a sweet female voice called.

Calvin turned on his heel at once and his jaw dropped when she saw Paloma emerge from the woods. Instead of her homespun linen dress, however, she wore a fringed avocado-green miniskirt and a long-sleeved pink blouse knotted over her navel. Paloma's fiery red curls framed her delicate face in a wild halo.

Calvin paused and glanced over his shoulder. "Paloma? Can it be?" He took a step towards her. "It's been, what, over thirty years! You haven't changed a bit," he marvelled. "How I've missed you, Paloma!"

"You sent me away, remember?" Paloma snapped. "After I told you I loved you, and you swore that you loved me, you told me to leave you alone. You said that your parents forbade you to see me anymore, and that they were sending you off to boarding school and then to college."

"But I came back and searched for you!" Calvin replied. "They were so adamant that I stay away from the woods, and so I did while they were alive. My mother was so sick, you know. Mother said it would break her heart if I ever set foot in that terrible place, and that there were horrible creatures within. Father let her have her say, although he told me I must always protect Prescott Woods."

"And a fine job you've done of that," interjected Brock. "Since when is selling a place equal to protecting it?"

"I make my own choices." Calvin jutted his jaw. "I refuse to be a prisoner in this decrepit house any longer. It's not fair." He scowled at Brock and Carmen. "Who are you people, anyway? What happened to the guy with the hurt ankle and the woman with the thick glasses?"

"Not fair?" a deep voice bellowed. Gavin strode from the woods and crossed his beefy arms over his chest. "Am I right in hearing you complain about the unfairness of this situation?" he thundered.

"Oh, shit, here we go," Carmen fretted.

"I am Gavin Rossi and all you see is mine. Your great-great-great-grandfather, Mack Prescott, owned a two-bit inn in a squalid village named Charade," Gavin growled. "I made a deal with him two hundred years ago. I would have this house" – he waved a meaty hand towards Prescott Manor – "built for him on the sole condition that he and his descendants would forever protect the adjoining woods and keep all intruders away." Gavin took three menacing steps towards Calvin, who swallowed noisily. "Your family was gifted with the finest home any mortals own in five states on one simple condition," he bellowed, "and you dare speak to me of unfair!"

Calvin raised his hands in a placating gesture. "Look, sir," he said. "My father did tell me to protect the woods, but he didn't tell me anything about an ancient family obligation to do so. And my mother," he continued, "was afraid of the place. I think she'd have left given any opportunity, but she didn't want to leave my father and me." He turned to Paloma. "I searched for you after Mother died and Father was killed in the car accident," he said. "I walked through the woods calling for you, but you never answered. Every time I entered, I barely escaped with my life. I was chased by a bear and hounded by a hawk. I even fell into a nest of rattlesnakes. Once a badger that must have been rabid ran after me." He shuddered. "After weeks of near-death scrapes in the woods with no response from you, I gave up, Paloma. I'm sorry. I shouldn't have listened to my parents when it came to the woods and to us. I should have trusted myself and trusted you."

Gavin turned his massive head to Paloma. "And you have something to answer for as well, daughter," he said in a quiet voice. "You pledged your love to a mortal? I have permitted casual dalliances for you children, but they are not to go beyond that, for your own safety."

Paloma raised her chin. "I did, Father, it's true," she admitted. "But only that once. I learnt then that people outside our family cannot be believed." She glared at Calvin.

The sounds of Korbin's and Lowell's footsteps preceded them as they joined the group.

Gavin raised one hand for silence. "Calvin Prescott, perhaps I can shed light on a few things. I've walked this earth for two centuries, but I confess that I am at times a foolish man. Your mother was a beautiful and sweet woman. When your father brought her to Prescott Manor, she was just nineteen years old. She would walk in the back garden and even explore the woods a bit. She was an avid birdwatcher"—he chuckled—"and so I would cast a glamour so as to appear to be a rare bird of some sort or other. I lured her into the woods just so I could be near her. She brought me happiness I hadn't felt since my own Maria left us." His mouth was set in a grim line. "It was wrong of me, I see now, but I thought I could convince her to leave your father and come away with me into the woods. One day I showed my true form to her and revealed some of the magic of Prescott Woods to her. Far from being enchanted, she was terrified. She ran from me and never set foot on the back lawn again. In my humiliation, I forbid all magic folk to come near the manor."

Calvin whistled. "Well, that explains a lot."

"In the generations prior to your parents'," Gavin mused, "there existed a certain symbiosis between Prescott Manor, Prescott Woods, Castle Speranza and the town of Charade. We of the woods knew the mortals of Prescott Manor, and we enlisted the aid of the magic folk in the manor's upkeep. Prescott Manor was not locked and guarded. Only the woods were off-limits to mortals. Townsfolk came to festivals and banquets at the Manor. It was the social centre of Charade. We of the woods traded our own elf-wrought goods with your store-bought clothes and foods."

"And chicken eggs," Paloma added.

"It seems to me that there exists an advantage in cooperation between those who abide in Prescott Woods, Prescott Manor, Castle Speranza and Charade. Would you agree, Calvin Prescott?"

"I would welcome both cooperation and company, Gavin Rossi," Calvin stated. "I will halt all plans to sell and develop Prescott Woods with the understanding that you and the folk of the woods will provide me with help in the manor's upkeep." He cast hopeful eyes on Paloma. "And I'll hope for friendly company as well." Paloma's face registered no emotion as she silently looked away.

Chapter Thirteen

Six months later…

Dora placed a last long blossom of green Bells of Ireland in the enormous arrangement and stepped back to admire it. Rich plum chrysanthemums, lime-green spider mums, purple salvia and delicate sweet lavender filled the deep glass pot. Dora had used fresh green acorns to fill the bottom of the pot, and the vibrant colour contrast was stunning.

"It looks fabulous, Dora," Carmen praised. "I knew you'd come up with something gorgeous for the first annual Prescott Fall Festival."

"Thanks, Carmen." Dora smiled. "I guess I've learnt a thing or two in fifteen years of running Bohemian Rhapsody. My B&B guests appreciate fresh flower arrangements, you know. And speaking of fabulous — damnation, girl! You look like you're ten years younger! I mean, you've always been beautiful, but you look amazing since you've been spending so much time out here. There must be something in the water here at Prescott Manor, huh?"

"Uh, I guess so." Carmen flushed and made a mental note to put an aging glamour on herself when out with mortal friends. It wouldn't do if she remained at the height of her youth and beauty while everyone around her continued to age.

Dora crossed her arms over her silk kimono robe and deepened the crevice of her already-impressive cleavage. "Thank you so much for making all this happen, Carmen. You're a miracle worker, girl! You talked Old Man Prescott out of selling the woods and you even got him to open up the manor to the town, like in the old days." She swept an admiring gaze over the fabulous décor of the entry room. "I mean, look at this place! I expected it to be amazing, but this goes beyond my wildest dreams!"

"It is spectacular, isn't it, Dora?" Carmen agreed. Of course, Dora knew nothing about the countless hours of elven labour that had been required to bring Prescott Manor back to its former glory. The Prescott Woods elves had repaired, reupholstered, painted, buffed and decorated like mad during the last months. Their tireless work had been a marvel to behold, Carmen thought, although it was just as impressive to see gruff, authoritarian Gavin bend to one knee to thank each and every elf for his or her hard work. In the back gardens, replanted by the gnomes, dragonflies, butterflies, hummingbirds and bluebirds swooped among the blooms while chipmunks and squirrels darted among the stone statuary. Carmen was pleased to see the real forms of the glamoured creatures in shadowy outlines. It was only fitting that the gnomes, tree spirits and elves were here to enjoy the party, too. Carmen even caught a whiff of trolls in the air and knew that the shy, lumbering creatures were hanging back unseen in the woods.

"The biggest miracle of all, though, is that you now live on Prescott property. You still haven't explained how that came about, Carmen," Dora scolded. At the far end of the lawn, Carmen's new cottage stood. It straddled the edge of the woods and the plush lawn of Prescott Manor. Like the Manor and Castle Speranza, the cottage had been built with troll, gnome, and elven hands and looked as though it had been there forever.

"Well, there's really nothing to tell," Carmen replied. "Calvin was more than willing to have a tenant to help him with legal odds and ends, as well as with upkeep of the manor. I sold my house to help fund the building of this new one, and here we are."

Dora shook her head in disbelief. "Yes, but how —"

"Ladies! It's time!" Beth burst into the room in a swirl of fuchsia silk and a tinkle of beads. Her auburn bangs fell over the colour-coordinated headband across her forehead. At her heels was Monica, her daughter, similarly clad in a matching, beaded bra, belt, and skirt set. Monica, however, had chosen royal blue to accent her honey-blonde hair and blue eyes. Bernice and Deb entered from the glass French doors that led to the lawn. Grey-haired Bernice, the Charade librarian, sparkled in lavender, while carrot-top Deb showed off her slender curves in a forest-green ensemble.

"Wait for me!" Colby called out. Her sleek blonde hair blew back from her face as she raced to join the group. Colby had chosen a rich shade of rose for her belly-dancing costume. Black-haired Dora whipped off her kimono to reveal her wine-red outfit. It magnificently accented her lush breasts and nipped her waist and full hips. Carmen wore her birthday gift from half a year ago — the lovely bronze belly-dancing attire that her friends had given her. Carmen did a mental count of her dancing troupe—Beth, Monica, Bernice, Deb, Dora and Colby. "We're missing one. Come on, slowpoke!" she directed to the shuffling footsteps in the hall.

Paloma, her wild flame-red hair billowing over her bare shoulders, ran in breathlessly with mint-green chiffon trailing behind her. "Sorry," she explained, blushing. "I...got caught up in something."

From upstairs, Carmen heard a distinct crash, followed by Calvin's unmistakable cursing. She glared at Paloma. "Honestly, haven't you tormented that poor man enough?"

"I don't know what you're talking about, Carmen," Paloma snickered. "And besides, can I help it if he's clumsy?"

Calvin thumped down the winding staircase and into the foyer. "Damnedest thing," he grumbled. "I'd swear I had put that vase on the table where it belonged, but there it was, right in front of my door, just waiting to get smashed." He gave Paloma a curious look, but she tossed her coppery curls and looked away. "Anyway, I don't want to miss the show, Carmen, so I'll deal with the broken vase later. Break a leg, ladies." Calvin went outside to join the seated gathering of mortal Charade residents and the fluttering and scampering glamoured audience of Prescott Woods inhabitants.

The Masked Charaders, a live band that specialised in belly-dance music, was seated to one side of the performers' wooden dance floor. The band, although somewhat hastily assembled, had proven to be a vast improvement over Carmen's Middle Eastern CD collection. Korbin had been thrilled to learn about the music and culture of the Middle East. He'd spent countless hours at the Charade library with Bernice, poring over the history and significance of various instruments before choosing his favourite. He played the *Dumbek*, a goblet-shaped drum that provided the rhythm to the songs. Marcus, Deb's husband and co-owner of Tie-Dyed and Gone to Heaven, had played clarinet in college, so it had been relatively easy for him to master the *Zumara*, a type of double clarinet. Paul Treble, one-time bagboy at Bushel and a Peck and current officer of the Charade Police Force, was the biggest surprise. Paul had taken to the *Kanoun* — a stringed instrument with a sound similar to a harp's — like a duck to water. Carmen suspected that his interest in producing belly-dancing music stemmed largely from a desire to get closer to Monica, Beth's daughter. Though Monica was now a freshman at Eastern Kentucky University, Carmen had seen her strolling with the earnest police officer during weekend visits home.

Korbin, Marcus, and Paul picked up their instruments and the sensual sounds of Middle Eastern music floated over Prescott Manor. Carmen and the rest of her troupe slid their fingers through the loops on their *Zills* and slithered out of the French doors one by one. They clapped their golden finger cymbals and rolled their hips in perfect, provocative rhythm.

Carmen spied Brock in the front row sitting next to Gavin. Lowell had an aisle seat on the other side of his father. She was relieved to see the three men beside each other, their past conflicts apparently resolved. Lowell kept one calloused hand on Dax's golden coat as he watched the show. Carmen felt a pang of jealousy, but she knew that Dax and Lowell made a great partnership. The sweet, loyal Lab had softened Lowell's thorny disposition somewhat, and Carmen had witnessed first-hand how much Dax enjoyed exploring the woods with him. Carmen also couldn't help but notice how Lowell appeared transfixed by Dora's curvaceous figure. He leant forwards in his seat and licked his lips as he watched Dora's plump, smooth thighs wiggle and sway.

Carmen moved through the practiced steps easily and stole a glance at Gavin, the stern patriarch of the clan. Like Lowell, he'd seemed to soften a bit, but he was much harder for her to read. He seemed uncertain at times about his changing place in the woods, although she knew he'd never give voice to any insecurities. With the new influences and new connections to the outside world, perhaps Gavin felt threatened, Carmen mused. She shimmied in a watercolour wash of bronze silk and arched into a deep backbend.

The last months had been a flurry of building and planning. Along with the renovations to Prescott Manor and the construction of her own small but luxuriant cottage, Castle Speranza itself had undergone an outdoor facelift. Carmen had supervised an enlargement of the chicken coop and raised some chicks in a hatchery to add to her flock of egg-layers. Paloma, although still prickly at times, had warmed over their discussions about the chickens. Spare Tire now followed Paloma about like a star-crossed, strutting lover through the newly planted flower gardens around the castle.

And where had Brock been during these months, Carmen wondered as she balanced a sword on her head during a dramatic portion of the programme. She eased her body through breathtaking contortions around the sword and smiled when she heard the smattering of impressed applause. She'd seen him, certainly, at Castle Speranza, when she and Paloma had met with the elves about the changes to the chicken coop. She'd caught glimpses of him while she'd been busy at her new home and while she'd advised Calvin about needed work at Prescott Manor. However, he'd been absent from her personal life. Perhaps that was a good thing.

Carmen joined her fellow dancers in the whirling, dizzying finale. Fuchsia, royal blue, lavender, forest green, rose, red, bronze and mint green swayed and rolled like chiffon waves in an ocean of bare arms, shoulders, stomachs and backs.

The breathless, glowing women took their bows at the end of the dance. Carmen indicated the musicians with a grateful round of applause. Korbin beamed as he stood with his fellow musicians and congratulated the dancers on their show. To Carmen, he seemed truly aglow for the first time.

Calvin stood and formally welcomed everyone to Prescott Fall Festival. He pointed out the tables with drinks and food and the booths with games of skill. Recorded Middle Eastern music began to play next to the dance floor. "And our own Carmen Foster," he said loudly, "will commence with free belly-dancing lessons for any who'd like to learn more."

Chapter Fourteen

The evening had passed in a haze of dancing, drinking and laughing. Somehow, Dora had managed to convince Lowell to join her onstage for a hip shimmy how-to, but it took just one hearty guffaw from Gavin to send his oldest child storming away in embarrassment.

After the last of the paper lanterns had been extinguished and the last guest had pulled from the driveway, Carmen said goodnight to Calvin and headed to her new cottage.

After living there for just one month, the slate-roofed stone cottage already felt like home. Carmen drew a steaming bath in the claw-footed tub, mentally thanking the elves for their addition of Healing Waters to her own plumbing—not that she didn't enjoy visiting the underground spring next to Castle Speranza—but Carmen appreciated a private soak. The lace-covered picture window in the bathroom faced the woods. Carmen turned off all of the lights and opened the drapes. Her sweat-dampened costume fell to the floor with a tired tinkly thump. She pumped some warm Living Earth from the cleverly designed elven spigot and plastered her face, shoulders, and arms with the delicately scented stuff. She felt it melt into her pores and ease her tired muscles. Carmen tested the bath with one toe before slipping into the soothing, fragrant heat.

Instantly, the magic liquid soaked through her skin and through her body, infusing her once more with the life-giving strength of the Healing Waters. With an effervescent heat, the water trickled into her blood and bones. She felt it strengthening and invigorating her. Carmen smiled and sank lower into the tub.

The gnomes had enlarged the bathing cavern next to Castle Speranza, and the elves had added some of their own improvements. There was now a screened area with an additional hot tub and mud bath in addition to the public ones. The cavern also included a steam shower, dry sauna and lounge area. The gnomes and elves frequented the spot, although they also continued to use their own temporary access points to the Healing Waters and Living Earth. Mephita, now a bit of celebrity in the gnome community, held court in the original mud bath. Surrounded by wide-eyed gnome admirers, she described how she'd rescued Brock from death then had gone on to save all of Prescott Woods.

Carmen didn't begrudge Mephita her fame a bit— she'd earned every bit of it. Carmen let her eyes slip shut and basked in the success of the Prescott Fall Festival. It was truly magical to see the denizens of Prescott Wood mingle with the mortals of Charade in an evening of fun and laughter. She'd secretly hoped to spend a few moments with Brock. He was a spoilt, self-centred child, true, but in her heart of hearts, Carmen missed his mirth-filled blue eyes and his warm caramel skin against her own. Perhaps, after her stern rebuke, he'd lost his taste for her.

"Such a shame," she murmured, "since he tasted so very good."

Mrrrrrr-owwwww!

Carmen sat up in the tub, her heart pounding. A wave sloshed over the side and onto a sleek orange tabby seated on the tiles. "Oh," Carmen said softly. "Hello, kitty. I thought you might be someone else." The cat blinked its green eyes and purred.

"Hold on and I'll find you some tuna in the kitchen." Carmen slid down in the tub and submerged her head. She massaged her scalp vigorously and scrubbed her face and shoulders clean before lifting her head from the steaming liquid and pulling the plug in her tub.

She stood, water streaming down her body, and ruffled her dripping locks. Stepping onto a mat, Carmen raised a towel to her face to blot it dry. Her skin thrummed with sensitivity and heightened energy from her soak.

She felt a soft tickle at her calf and caught her breath. Surely just the cat's tongue, but weren't cats' tongues scratchy and rough? She held the towel over her eyes and waited, heart pounding.

The silky touch flickered at her ankle like the most delicate of kisses, then traced up the damp skin on the side of her knee. Carmen felt two small, velvety pads of pressure beneath her knee. Were they a cat's front paws, or a man's fingers?

She bit her lip and squeezed her eyes closed. "Kitty, are you thirsty?" she asked. She felt a sharp nip above her knee and cried out in surprise. "Kitty!" she scolded. "No need for that, I'll take care of you."

Carmen felt the two points of contact move around her knee to the inside of her leg before tracing their way up her inner thigh. Clearly, this was no cat.

Carmen dropped the towel to the floor and lowered her hands to the tousled head between her legs. "I am thirsty, now that you mention it," a familiar male voice growled, "but I think I've found just what I want to drink."

He eased her down onto the curved side of the tub and spread her knees wide. Carmen twisted her fingers through his ash-grey hair and sighed happily. He sucked the water from her plump pussy lips and brushed his stubbled cheeks over the heat-softened skin between her legs. "I can look like anything, you know," he whispered, "a fluffy grey cat, a racoon, an elderly geologist, a sleek tabby cat—but it's always me, Carmen. You know that." He pushed the tip of his tongue inside her cunt and held it, tasting her as slow seconds ticked by.

"Yes, I do know that," Carmen murmured. "I suppose I—ah!" she cried out. Brock wound his arms beneath her thighs and pushed his tongue far into her pussy. She exhaled through pursed lips and arched her back. "I suppose I lost track of that for a moment, or maybe I was trying not to get my hopes up."

Brock pulled his tongue out and flicked it over the damp, swollen nub of her clit, then slid one slender finger inside her. Carmen felt dizzy with impatience and desperate for a deep fucking, but willed herself to focus on the pleasure of the moment. "You were so beautiful tonight, Carmen," he murmured.

She whimpered softly and imagined how his cock was growing thicker and harder by the second. "It's going to feel so good when you push it in," she whispered.

"Yes, it will, Carmen," he agreed, and added a second finger.

Carmen raised her hands to her bare breasts and found her nipples. "It's been a long time," she noted, and rolled each stiff nipple between her fingertips. "I thought you weren't going to come around."

"You told me I was a self-centred child," Brock answered. He withdrew his hand, lifted her from the edge of the tub down onto the fluffy bath mat, then lowered his hips between her thighs. "You said I needed to grow up."

"Oh," Carmen breathed. The silky-hard tip of his erection nudged against her opening.

"You were right," he continued. Carmen felt faint as his shaft eased its way within. She closed her eyes, blind to all sensation except the beautifully brutal way his cock stretched her entrance.

"I know I've had an unconventional life, Carmen," he said, penetrating farther. "I know I've got a lot to learn."

Carmen nodded, too overwhelmed by sensation to speak.

"I'm trying, though," he added. "I've been learning about the gnomes and the elves, spending time with them. I've learnt about the trolls and tree-spirits, too. Turns out trolls aren't so stupid after all."

"That's good, Brock," Carmen forced out. She widened her thighs to take him deeper.

"And we—Paloma, Lowell and even Korbin—have been being more assertive with Father. He understands that we're adults now. It's different than it was at Castle Speranza." Brock lowered his face to Carmen's breast and sucked one erect nipple into his mouth.

"I know that you are an independent woman, Carmen, and that's why I've given you your space." Brock's hips began to pump faster into Carmen's. He lifted her knees up to her ribs and slammed his cock deeply into her. Carmen cried out in mingled pain and relief.

She ran her fingernails down his corded back and scraped hard. Brock growled and fucked harder, pummelling her into the tile floor. Carmen's orgasm began at that sweet point where the tip of his erection touched her inner walls and exploded from there. She gave a guttural cry, and wrapped her ankles around his back. As the spasms from her climax began to wane, the thick surge of Brock's cum inside her brought them back to full strength.

Long moments later, he lay panting on her chest, his face buried between her bare tits. "Glorious," he breathed.

"Amazing," Carmen agreed.

As his heartbeat returned to normal, Brock eased back on his heels and gazed at Carmen, stretched nude on the floor before him. "You're everything to me, Carmen," he told her. "You're vital and smart and beautiful and independent. I'd never take any of that away."

Carmen smiled, adoring every inch of him—the rich gem-blue of his eyes, the wild grey fluff of his hair and the sculpted caramel gorgeousness of his body.

"What I'd like you to know is that I'm having the gnomes and elves construct a cottage for me between yours and Castle Speranza. I've put in a request for my own bath of Healing Waters and my own conduit to the Living Earth. I don't want to take away your independence, Carmen, but I do want to love you. I want to visit you, and for you to visit me. I want to explore the woods and the town with you, and experience whatever parts of your long life you're willing to share with me. I don't want all of you, Carmen." He took her hand and kissed her knuckles. "Just those parts of you that can love me as much as I love you."

He closed his eyes and exhaled. "But only if that's what you choose, Carmen."

Carmen pulled her hand away and sat up. She took his playful, lovable face between her hands. "Yes, Brock, I want you to have the parts of me that love you, although I warn you, those parts will only grow and get stronger. I want you to be part of my days and nights. I want us to learn and grow together in these unconventional, amazing lives we have in Prescott Woods. I want to love you." She pulled him close to her for a kiss of promise and hope.

"Brock, I choose it."

BEDS AND BLAZES

Dedication

For James and for motorcycle rides through the
Appalachians, where ancient magic hides behind
every twist in the road.

Prologue

"Are we all clear, then? I don't want there to be any confusion about this." Gavin spoke severely and looked at each person seated around the great oval table in turn. "Things are changing in Prescott Woods, and we need to ensure our safety and survival."

"Aye, aye, Father," Paloma answered and saluted crisply. "We are never to appear as humans in Charade. We must use glamours to disguise ourselves unless we are in the woods or at Prescott Manor." She tossed her fiery hair over her shoulder and tapped her fingers on the tabletop.

Gavin grunted and addressed his youngest son. "Korbin, you may continue your studies at the library for the time being, but I'd like for you to acquire the books you want for the library at Castle Speranza. Within a couple of months, halt all visits to the Charade Public Library and conduct all of your studies here." He cleared his throat awkwardly. "Please."

His fair-haired youngest child nodded silently.

"No human is to enter the woods for any reason. If a mortal sets foot in Prescott Woods, we are to use glamours to frighten that person away," Brock added.

"Correct, son. Be sure to enlist the aid of gnomes, elves, trolls and any other of the magic beings that are close by. It's in their best interests to keep the secrets of Prescott Woods safe." Gavin turned to Carmen. "You, Carmen, have perhaps the most difficult task of any of us. You must negotiate your roles with care, being certain to wear an ageing glamour around humans so that your immortal condition remains hidden. You must also refrain at all costs from arousing suspicion from anyone you know in town. Please continue to conduct your dance classes and law practice in the wing of Prescott Manor that Calvin has set aside for you, and limit your excursions to Charade to no more than one or two per month."

Carmen caught his gaze. "I understand, Gavin."

Gavin stood and placed his broad palms on the table. "Understand this, too, children. You may find yourselves in a delicate position. You are all adults — most of you have been adults for two centuries — and it's entirely natural that you seek out a mate to share your days."

"Father!" Lowell interrupted. "This is hardly the time or the place — "

"It's the perfect time and place, son! Let me finish," Gavin snapped.

Lowell crossed his beefy arms over his chest and listened.

"I want you all to be happy and to have companionship, but more than that, I insist that we keep the woods safe for all those who live here. The Fair Folk, the gnomes, the elves, the tree spirits, the trolls and every magical being here deserves to exist in peace. We cannot guess and hope when it comes to our survival. We must be *certain*. Therefore, I insist that, should you find a person you wish to bring into our fold, that person must agree to relocate permanently to Prescott Woods *before* you divulge our secrets. I will not tempt humans with immortality and then ask them to commit to our ways."

Gavin's voice deepened to an ominous rumble. "Only if a human will commit to leaving everything he or she knows in order to be with you may you invite that human to partake of the Healing Waters and Living Earth. If that scenario sounds near-impossible, then I'm describing it perfectly. Our lives are bound forever to Prescott Woods and to each other. Adding another member to our family is a huge step. I demand that you show it the proper gravity. We cannot permit sneaky or accidental conversion of human to Fair Folk" — he glowered at Brock — "and we cannot risk revealing the magic in the woods to one who is not part of it."

Silence fell. "Paloma, Korbin? Can you abide by this? Brock and Carmen?" One by one, all agreed, rose and left the room.

Gavin sighed and clapped his oldest son on the shoulder. "You've always been my sturdiest, most trustworthy child," he told Lowell. "Always had your feet firmly planted on the ground. I know I can count on you to help me keep the secret of Prescott Woods safe from outsiders, Lowell."

Chapter One

"Are you, like, banging Calvin Prescott on the side or something?" Dora asked. "Because I will never understand how you talked him into this, Carmen." She walked around the perimeter of the gazebo and clicked her tongue in admiration. "It's like something out of a magazine," she noted, "but then, I guess the manor it's attached to is nothing to sneeze at." The wisteria that grew over the breezeway was in full show and ruffled purple blooms hung down over the walkway like dozens of Chinese lanterns.

"Well, Calvin thought it was a great idea. He's all for increasing his property value, and the pergola breezeway and this gazebo definitely do that. Besides, I'm pretty sure he got a great deal on labour and materials from some folks he knows." Carmen cleared her throat. "It'll be perfect for my belly dancing lessons, but it's also a lovely place to entertain, don't you think?"

The breezeway arched around the back garden of the manor, past plantings of lavender dwarf irises, frilly white rhododendrons and lilac orchids interspersed among beds of hardy Kentucky wildflowers. "It's stunning," Dora agreed. "Good on Calvin for using plants native to the area, too. That man has a green thumb as big as a house. I've never seen such prolific poppies and trumpet creepers."

"Calvin offered some input, of course, but it's Calvin's gardener who's the real genius. Bufo is a treasure."

"'Bufo'. That's an odd name," Dora noted. "Doesn't it mean 'toad'?" She turned to Carmen with a puzzled expression, but her friend offered no explanation. "Whatever his name is, I'd love for him to help me with the beds around Bohemian Rhapsody. They're nice, but I'd love for Bufo to come work his magic on them."

Carmen made a choking sound then dropped to her knees to turn on her stereo. Sensual Middle Eastern music filled the air. "I'm afraid Bufo only works on Prescott property, Dora," she said briskly. "But I'll be sure to pass on the compliment. Are you ready to get some dancing in?" She pulled off her sweatshirt and pants to reveal a charcoal jog bra and fitted Lycra capris, then tied on her coin-covered hip sash.

"Sure thing, coach," Dora answered. She stripped off her day clothes and donned her hip scarf as well. "You're sure Calvin's gone, right? Nobody's here to see us?" She rubbed her upper arms self-consciously and glanced towards the manor. The air was slightly cool, but she knew that activity would warm her quickly.

"You look beautiful, Dora. I'd love to have curves like yours. Men are totally crazy about them. But yes, Calvin's gone and there's no one in the house that I know of. I need to see the outline of your body during our lessons, so it's good that you're wearing fitted clothes." Carmen handed a plastic tray to Dora and grinned. "Ready to practise balancing? You're gonna love dancing with a tray on your head, especially when you get to create a flower arrangement to go on it."

Surrounded by the fragrant plantings and serene grounds of Prescott Woods, Dora centred the tray atop her head and followed Carmen's instructions. Rolling her hips and sinuously waving her arms, she relaxed and felt the warm, sensual strength that enveloped her during Middle Eastern dancing.

From an oak tree at the edge of the woods, a bluebird flew towards the gazebo. Although its wings beat quickly, the bird's path switched back and forth so that its progress was slow compared to other birds. "Oh my gosh," Dora breathed when it landed on the white-painted rail of the gazebo. The plastic tray clattered to the floor next to her, but the bird didn't budge. "We have an audience, Carmen! I love bluebirds — they're so sweet and cheerful!"

"Yeah, well, I'm sure it's just here for the flowers and bugs, Dora. There are lots of birds in the woods." Carmen narrowed her eyes at the brilliant blue animal. She started to make a shooing gesture, but Dora caught her hand.

"It's not hurting anything," she said. "I kind of like having someone to dance for, even if it's just a bird. It sort of reminds me of that grey cat that used to hang out in the window of the studio in town. Remember him, Carmen?"

Carmen grunted and handed Dora her dropped tray. "Okay, you win," she agreed. "Today we dance for a feathered audience member. All I can say is, he'd better not poop on the gazebo or I'm going after a broom."

The bird ruffled its feathers and warbled sweetly as Dora once more followed Carmen's dance instructions.

Lowell rested his chin on the gazebo rail and took a deep breath. Dora was, simply put, the most stunning woman to ever grace the planet. That long, thick, raven hair, that upturned nose, those lips that managed to be both full and delicate at the same time... And that body! By three hells, he hadn't known a figure like that was possible. Muscular and firm, yet yielding and soft in the places it mattered most, and with a bosom and hips to make any red-blooded man weak in the knees.

He tipped his head to one side and watched her hips pivot and her full breasts tremble with each step. Carmen, of course, was watching and was far from impressed, but she was powerless to stop him. Dora would be horrified if she chased off a sweet little bluebird. He chuckled and cast his gaze lower, to Dora's plump thighs, rounded calves and tender, delicate feet. A rampant erection jutted from his crotch, but he was far too used to walking around in the nude to care. Carmen had seen it all before, and it was worth a smidgeon of exposure to be able to behold Dora up close. He whistled appreciatively.

"Awww," Dora cooed. "He's tilting his little head and singing along with the music. I think he likes me." She executed a turn and a deep knee bend, all while keeping the tray on its precarious perch. "See? I do better with an audience, Carmen."

Carmen's movements became jerky and her own tray clattered to the floor. "You can keep practising," she said in a terse voice. "I'm going to get something for us to drink. I think it's getting a little warm out here."

Dora continued to dance, stepping forward and backward, dipping her hips down and moving her head from side to side. Smiling, she moved closer to the bluebird. Lowell thought he would die from pleasure overload. Dora undulated before his very eyes, shaking those gorgeous breasts scant inches from his face. How he wanted to drop his glamour, grab her in his arms and carry her off into the woods... *It's something Brock might have done,* he thought, *but I'm stronger than that.*

He craned his neck and caught a whiff of her fragrance — some sweet flower or other — glorious. He watched, entranced, as her nipped waist swayed over those lush hips and her belly undulated with rippling precision. The head of his erect cock bumped against the lattice walls of the gazebo and Lowell groaned with desire. A brief look told him that Carmen was still inside, so he was unobserved... He took his shaft in his hand and slid it through his fist. His flesh grew tighter as he rubbed it. *I'm going to have to touch her,* he decided. *There's just no way around it.*

The side door to the manor shut with a bang and the sound of approaching footsteps emanated from the breezeway, but Lowell was too far gone to notice. Dora danced for him seductively, as though she knew that he was hiding behind the face of an innocent little bluebird. He imagined sliding his erection between the crevice of Dora's sweat-sheened breasts, pushing them together with his palms so that her warm flesh enveloped his cock completely.

"Can I interest you in some ice water?" he heard Carmen ask brightly. Dora turned just as Carmen lunged forward with her tray in a theatrically clumsy stumble. She let the plastic tray fall, but caught the pitcher. Lowell didn't have time to duck when he saw the torrent of ice cubes and water flying through the air at him. The frigid mixture splashed over his head and ran over his bare back, chest and aching shaft.

"Shit, that's cold!" he sputtered, stepping away from the gazebo to brush the freezing water from his skin.

"Ummm... Did that bird just...talk?" Dora whispered. She raised her hand to her throat and took one step away from the feathered blue terror.

Sputtering, Lowell locked eyes with a heartily amused Carmen before running back into the safety of Prescott Woods.

Chapter Two

Later that evening, Carmen was reading *Belly Dancing Quarterly* magazine and kicking back with a cup of homemade cocoa, enhanced with a generous pour of heavy cream, and a slice of pistachio-crusted cheesecake. She had determined to her delight that the Healing Waters and the Living Earth not only provided health and longevity, but also an enviable eat-anything-and-keep-your-figure diet plan.

Thank heaven for magical subterranean spas, she thought happily.

Outside her front door was the immaculate and mundane back lawn of Prescott Manor, and out the back were the shadowy enchanted trees of Prescott Woods. Carmen's cottage, built with labour from elves, gnomes and trolls, had one foot in each world, just like her.

"Does she be needin' anything more?" a raspy female voice asked.

"No, I'm all set, Limax. The house looks terrific. Thank you so much for cleaning it again. The flowers on the table are gorgeous, too."

The gnome bobbed her head and tittered. "Oh, she knows how I like to be useful and such, so it's my pleasure, it is." Limax beamed, exposing a mouth full of crooked and discoloured teeth, and Carmen saw that she was tearing up again. Like her namesake, the slug, Limax was prone to gooey secretions, especially when she became emotional. Carmen had taught her to carry a fresh handkerchief to wipe her streaming eyes and runny nose. Considering that she had a housekeeper who wanted to be paid in praise alone, putting up with a little mucus was no big deal.

Sniffling, Limax shuffled out and left her to her dessert. Moments later, Carmen heard a knock on the back door. "Come in," she sang out. "Babe, you have got to try this cheesecake that Dora brought me — it's to die for." Carmen looked up, but instead of seeing Brock, her boyfriend, she saw none other than his stocky, scowling brother.

As one of the Fair Folk herself, Carmen hadn't been fooled by Lowell's bluebird guise for a minute, but she could see now that he had dropped it entirely. The phantasmic bird outline had vanished, and only a six-and-a-half foot tower of irritable male remained. She was, however, relieved to see that he had put on real clothes. Dealing with a pissed-off Lowell was bad enough, but a pissed-off, naked Lowell was more than she could handle.

As had become his custom, Lowell wore a kilt. Ever since he'd learned that a Scottish/Italian designer had come up with an Italian national tartan, he'd taken to a kilt like a wood duck to the Castle Speranza pond. Even though Carmen preferred lanky, lean men, she had to admit that Lowell looked awfully good in the blue and black tartan and snug rugby shirt. He had the bulky, muscular body of a lumberjack and, at present, the dangerous expression of a hungry grizzly bear.

"Hi, Lowell," Carmen said. She gave him an uneasy grin. "Want some cheesecake?"

"I do not." He crossed his beefy arms over his chest. "I don't appreciate you dousing me with ice water, Carmen. That was extremely unpleasant." He stared at her and the muscles in his jaw clenched.

"Yeah, well," Carmen replied, "I don't appreciate you showing up naked and, like, rubbing yourself while Dora and I were dancing." She shuddered. "Lowell, that's just *gross*. You're practically my brother."

He shifted from foot to foot and Carmen thought she detected rising colour in his cheeks. *Good,* she thought with annoyance. *He should be embarrassed.*

"I, ah, regret that I partook in, uh, licentious behaviour in front of you," Lowell stammered. "It was not gentlemanly of me. However —"

"Have you been putting the moves on my girl?" Lowell turned as Brock entered the kitchen. "Back off, Lowell. This one's all mine." Brock bent to kiss Carmen on the lips and took the seat next to her at the table.

"Here, honey, have some." Carmen lifted a fork with a bite of cheesecake to Brock's lips. He closed his eyes as he chewed and swallowed, then bobbed his head in appreciation. "Damn, that's good! Did Dora make that?" Brock looked up at Lowell, still standing and stewing before them. "Have you had a piece of this? If not, you're missing out, man."

Lowell grunted irritably and eyed the cheesecake. "Dora made it?" he asked in a quiet voice. "It's good?"

Carmen chuckled and stood to get a plate, fork and napkin for him. Minutes later, Lowell had silently devoured his slice of cheesecake and sat before Brock and Carmen with a noticeably less sour expression. "She's a good cook too," he whispered. "Amazing."

"Lowell, you are ridiculous. You can't act like it's horrible for Fair Folk to date humans when you clearly are lusting after one yourself. Do you even remember how you freaked out when Brock brought me to Castle Speranza? You were a nutcase."

"That was a long time ago, Carmen," Lowell protested, "and things have changed between the Fair Folk and humans in town."

"Is that so? Are you sure that Father would agree with you, Lowell?" interjected Brock.

"He ought to," Lowell muttered. "But that doesn't mean I want to talk about it to him just yet."

Carmen lifted Brock's hand and kissed his knuckles before continuing. "My point is—why don't you ask her out on a date like a normal person, Lowell? Obviously, you're not a normal person." Brock guffawed and Carmen studiously ignored him. "She doesn't have to know that, though, Lowell. You don't have to lurk around and stalk the poor woman, and you certainly don't have to pretend to be one of Snow White's woodland pals to get close to her."

"The bluebird glamour again?" Brock muttered.

"Yeah," Lowell admitted. "Chicks dig it." Brock gave a knowing nod.

Carmen sighed in exasperation. "Look, Dora's a nice, grown-up lady and, at over two hundred years old, you're hardly a child, Lowell. Just go talk to her. Sheesh. You Rossi boys are ridiculous."

Lowell stared at his beefy hands in his lap and shook his head. "She's just so beautiful, though. So sweet and smart and talented, and her body is"—he sighed—"unforgettable."

Carmen caught Brock's glance and shared a smile.

"I've been with the dryads and, on occasion, a Charade woman, but this is different. Dora's special. I don't know why she'd ever give me a second glance," Lowell concluded sadly. Outside, night had fallen in the woods. Dry branches crunched and snapped beneath Carmen's kitchen window.

"Just be yourself and it'll all work out," Carmen advised as she served him another piece of cheesecake. "Trust me."

* * * *

Dora put the finishing touches on a late spring arrangement for her entry table. Pink, magenta and chartreuse zinnias, blushing wild roses, white snapdragons and trailing variegated ivy filled her large entry vessel. *Homegrown,* she thought, *and fit for a queen.*

She moved through the six-thousand-five-hundred-square-foot Victorian house, locking up and turning off lights, and thought, *That pretty much describes my B&B.*

Dora felt a familiar rush of pride and happiness as she surveyed her home. *Bohemian Rhapsody is rated the number four bed and breakfast in Kentucky.* She smiled. *And for good reason. It's clean and comfortable, and guests love my sweet potato breakfast casserole, the floral themed rooms and the sun-dried linens.* Dora peeked into the Daffodil Suite and frowned when she saw that the wallpaper next to the light switch was peeling a bit. *Got to fix that tomorrow.* The Dogwood Suite was perfect, as were the Iris and Morning Glory Suites, thanks to unending vigilance on Dora's part. She needed an assistant, but that was completely out of the question, and Dora was proud and happy to toil away.

Bohemian Rhapsody was a living thing to her, a loyal friend and a dependent child, brought to life by her own determination and hard work. Each blemish in the ageing house might as well have been on Dora's own body, it troubled her so deeply. "Tomorrow, the gardens in the morning and the Dogwood wallpaper in the afternoon. Maybe I'll have time to polish the silver service."

Dora poured a glass of cabernet, blew out the rosemary-scented candle on the counter and prepared to retire to her bedroom, the Queen Anne's Lace master suite. Just as she reached to turn off the light, she noticed a mockingbird perched on the windowsill of her kitchen. It peered at her with alert black eyes and hopped on its clawed feet.

"What is it with the birds around here, anyway?" Dora chuckled.

Chapter Three

She rose at seven the next morning. The Mathesons weren't expected until eleven and the Parkers planned to check in at two, so there was plenty of time to get a little gardening in after she hung the sheets to dry.

Dora dressed in loose overalls and a T-shirt, stuffed her thick hair up into a wide-brimmed hat and donned her clogs and gloves. A riot of birdsong greeted her when she stepped outside and the bright May morning coaxed a smile to her face. The climbing roses, draped like a gem-studded stole down the side of the house, were almost garish in their ruby profusion. She knelt before the peonies, whose buds were about to burst with bright fuchsia petals, and started weeding. "I should really have divided these in the fall," she muttered, "but I reckon they'll make it one more summer."

Soon, she felt lulled into contentedness by the repetitive action and the immersion with nature. She began to sing a favourite Aretha Franklin song, 'Natural Woman', as she worked.

By the last line, Dora was overcome by the power of the Queen of Soul. She leant back on her heels, squeezed her eyes shut and belted out Aretha's heartfelt lyrics in a womanly growl.

And heard a quiet, distinctively male cough above her.

Dora lurched forward and looked up. A pair of huge booted feet, two bulky, hairy legs, a blue plaid skirt and, beside them, some pale gold paws greeted her eyes. The figure stepped back hastily, but not before Dora caught a glimpse of what was beneath the kilt. Those muscular legs stretched right on up to a gorgeous male package — semi-erect, thick and scrumptious.

"Oh my!" she gasped. "I didn't see you there. Hello!" She stood, blushing wildly, and wished she had on something a bit more figure-flattering than an old pair of overalls. "Paul Matheson, I presume?"

The man, who towered over her and looked like he could lift a VW bug with his bare hands, appeared painfully uncomfortable. "Um, no, I'm afraid not," he muttered.

Dora caught his eyes on her bosom — she knew its curves were clearly visible beneath her snug T-shirt — and he looked away swiftly. The golden lab next to him capered off and out of sight.

Dora drew her eyebrows together and stood. "Then it's Mr Parker, I suppose? Randy, is that correct?"

"No, madam, I'm not Randy," he replied.

Dora glanced downward, wondering what on earth this person was doing in her yard and whether she ought to start screaming bloody murder, when she saw that he was decidedly excited by their conversation. An erection, too impressive to ignore, tented the front of his kilt. "That is, I'm not Mr Parker,

I suppose you might see that I am somewhat, well..."
His voice trailed off miserably. He turned his back to
her and crossed his arms over his chest. The back of
his neck blazed a deep crimson hue. "I do apologise,
madam. I suppose I ought to be on my way."

He began to walk away, but Dora caught his arm
and stopped him. "It's okay," she chuckled. "It's
actually flattering, and I'll ignore it if you will. But
what can I do for you, Mr — ?"

"Mr Rossi," he supplied. "I'm Lowell Rossi."

"Oh, of course! I know you. I saw you at the Harvest
Festival last fall at the Prescott Manor. We danced
together for a minute or two. You look a little different
now, though. Maybe it's the beard, or possibly the
kilt," she mused. "Anyway, where have you been?
Have you been travelling? I've been to the manor
quite a few times with Carmen, and I came to the
Valentines' Ball, but I haven't seen you at all. I hope
you've not been sick?"

"Ah, well," he mumbled, "I've been here and there, I
suppose, but nowhere special. You, madam, are Dora,
is that correct?" He turned back to her and, with
effort, Dora avoided looking below his waist.

"Yes, Dora Fontaine." She took off her gloves and
offered him a hand. Lowell stared at it as though it
were an alien life form, then shook it firmly. Dora felt
a shuddery thrill at his grip — huge, callused and
warm, he held her as though she were made of glass.
It seemed like a hand that could uproot a tree and,
then next minute, cradle a baby bird.

"Won't you come in for some tea?" Dora asked. "If
you can forgive my appearance, that is. I'd love to
learn more about what you've been doing. Carmen is
always so mysterious about Brock's family."

He nodded silently. *A man of few words,* she thought, and led him inside. "Welcome to Bohemian Rhapsody!" Dora swept her arm to indicate the curving staircase, vintage wallpaper and stained glass chandelier. "It's no Prescott Manor, of course, but it's my own little dream come true. You can see I love flowers and vintage fabrics, and I collect all sorts of Victorian stuff, from dolls to greeting cards to hats. My guests enjoy perusing my displays, you know."

"It's very nice," Lowell replied. "Very floral and, ah, pretty, in a girly kind of way. I like it."

"Have a seat in the breakfast nook while I heat the kettle." Dora smiled to see his bulky form, redolent of testosterone and all things manly, ensconced on the yellow chintz cushions and framed by the crisp Battenberg curtains. "Do you like the smell of lilac?" she asked.

"Um, sure," he answered. "As in the flower?"

Dora lit a pale purple candle in a mason jar and set it on the table before him. "As in the scented candle. I'm in the habit of burning one when I have a bite to eat. Sort of makes me feel as though I've got cheerful company, even when I'm alone." The yellow flame danced on the table and a sweet floral fragrance permeated the room. "Plus it makes the place smell nice." She placed teabags in her pot—one mint, one orange, one lemon—and withdrew two cups and saucers from the cupboard. An array of vibrant cups and saucers glinted on the shelves. "I have an eclectic set of teacups," she said proudly. "Here are the Royal Alberts for you and the Crown Staffordshires for me. It's like drinking tea from a different bouquet every time, you know?"

Lowell picked up the dainty pink and green floral cup and nodded. "It's quite beautifully shaped," he said, deep voice rumbling. "Like you."

He met her gaze with an earnest expression, and Dora caught a glimpse of colour rising in his cheeks. The kettle screamed on the stove. "Oh!" Dora started. "Water's ready!" Heart pounding, she filled the teapot and brought it to the table, along with a squeeze bottle of honey, spoons, lacy napkins and a colourful tin box. "Lemon shortbread cookies?" she offered. "I made them myself."

Lowell accepted a cookie and chewed thoughtfully. "Perfection."

She removed her hat and fluffed her hair in the reflection in the stove door before joining him at the table. "I'm so pleased you like them." She sipped her tea and cleared her throat. "So, Lowell, what is it that you do? Some sort of land management for the woods? It's such a beautiful stretch of pristine woodland. We're certainly lucky to have Prescott Woods close by. It makes the whole area seem magical, don't you think?"

Lowell picked up another cookie and took a bite. He swallowed before answering. "Yes, that's exactly right, Dora. I keep tabs on the animals and plants of the woods and conduct some studies, too. It, ah, turns out there are some unusual species in Prescott Woods."

"Oh, you're a researcher? A biologist? How fascinating! Are you going to publish your findings?"

"Ah, well, it's possible, that is—"

Dora stood abruptly. Her mouth dropped open and she stared through the window behind Lowell's head. "What? Are those my sheets? What in the world...?

Excuse me, Lowell." Shouting indignantly, she hurried outside with Lowell on her heels.

A pile of sheets lay in a muddied heap and a lone pillowcase fluttered on the lawn near the corner. The feathered blond tail of a barking dog disappeared around the edge of the house. Sputtering indignantly, Dora darted to collect the pillowcase and ran to inspect her clothesline. Every clean sheet had been plucked from the cords and the folding table and laundry bin were toppled on their sides.

"Well, you could knock me over with a feather, Lowell Rossi. What kind of a dog yanks down sheets from the line? What in the world could have gotten into Dax? He never acted like that when he lived with Carmen." Her eyebrows scrunched and she shook her head. "I could have sworn I saw a bat for a second there, but I must be going crazy. Bats don't come out in the daytime." Dora exhaled and turned to the heap of damp cloth. "I'll have to rewash all my linens and just hope there are no tears or stains."

Lowell's eyes narrowed and a low grumble resounded in his throat. "Strange behaviour for a dog, all right," he scowled. Dax's vocalisations dwindled in the distance. Dora picked up the table to right it, and Lowell darted to her side. "No, let me," he insisted as he trotted over. "Don't strain yourself."

"It's perfectly all right," Dora chuckled, hoisting the piece of furniture up in the air. "I'm stronger than I look." As he reached for the table, Lowell tripped over the laundry hamper beside it and fell in an heap at Dora's feet. The table swung about overhead and Dora lost her balance. She fell squarely on top of Lowell's lap, her forehead resting on the wadded fabric of his kilt and her face squashed on Lowell's bared crotch.

"Wha — wha — wha — huh — " Dora stuttered. Lowell's beefy package, framed by a dusting of hair, pressed against her lips and nose. She struggled to lift her chest up from his lap, but his agitated squirming beneath her made it difficult. "Gah!" Dora pushed away from him at last and rocked back on the grass. "Sheesh!"

Lowell, long legs outspread like a splayed frog, yanked his kilt down and scrambled to his feet. His face, Dora noted, was an alarming shade of red. "Ah, my apologies, madam," he said. "How very awkward this is." He took a step backwards and scrubbed his fingers through his beard.

Dora stood and dusted herself off. "No harm done," she assured him. She tossed her hair over her shoulder and smiled. "You broke my fall nicely."

Lowell's cheeks darkened until they were almost purple. "Oh." He cleared his throat and dropped his gaze down to Dora's chest. Dora pressed her upper arms against the sides of her breasts to deepen her cleavage and cocked one eyebrow. "Oh!" Lowell stared, transfixed. Dora noted the growing bulge in the fabric of his kilt.

"Wanna come finish our tea?" Dora asked. "I can do the laundry later."

Lowell glanced back at the door. The front of his kilt lifted farther away from his body and the hemline drew up to mid-thigh. "Tea does sound nice," he answered. "I am fond of your cups, after all." He cleared his throat. "Ah, well, you know, the china ones, that is — "

"Hello-oo!" a female voice sang out. "Paul and Lucy Matheson here. Anybody home? Did we find the right place? We're a bit early."

A couple in identical royal blue tracksuits and black vinyl fanny packs emerged and stood next to Dora's budding peonies. "Is this Bohemian Rhapsody?" the woman asked. She caught a glimpse of Lowell, his erection undeniable, and elbowed her husband. "I think we're interrupting something, Paul," she chuckled in a stage whisper.

"Oh, arrggh, urrrm, well then," Lowell mumbled, sounding every bit the flummoxed pirate to Dora's ears. "I'd better be going." He lowered his head and started to slink past the chortling couple, then paused by the rose-festooned wall. Blushing fiercely, he plucked a bloom and placed it in Dora's hand with a stiff nod.

"It's a blaze rose," she told him. "They're my favourite." She tucked it behind her ear.

"Well, it's pretty, Dora," he said gruffly, "and, uh, it smells nice. Just like you." He waved awkwardly at the newly arrived couple before disappearing beyond the zinnias.

Dora sighed. "Welcome, Mr and Mrs Matheson. I'm so glad you arrived safely. I can show you your room, but unfortunately the bed isn't made yet. I pride myself on freshly washed linens for my guests, but my laundry had a run-in with a naughty puppy and will have to be rewashed. I'll have it ready in a couple of hours."

"No problem," the woman chirped. "We'll just drop off our bags and check out the town square. My friend Connie was raving about a shop there. Something about Tie Dyeing, I think?"

"Yes, yes, my friends Marcus and Deb own it. It's called 'Tie Dyed and Gone to Heaven'. You should check out Groovy Grounds, the coffee shop, and

Patchouli Pets, too. I heard they have a couplecouple of of rescue chinchillas available for adoption now."

"Oh, I just knew we'd love Charade!" She bounced on her toes and turned to her husband. "Thank you, honey bunny. Eskimo kiss!"

"Anything for you, turtle dove," the man replied. Dora watched as the man lowered his face to his wife's. Both shut their eyes, wrinkled their noses and rubbed the tips of their noses together.

Dora bit back a laugh, but beneath the amusement she felt a pang of jealousy. She showed the Mathesons to the Morning Glory room—*the flowers match their tracksuits, after all*—and returned to the backyard to gather up the dirty sheets.

* * * *

Lowell, seething, paused silently at the arched entrance to the bathing cavern. Above a tub of warm, liquid earth, a mud-crusted head, still as carved stone, leaned against the rim. Twisted locks of hair, also coated in a layer of silt, coiled like Medusa's snakes into the rippling contents of the pool. A brazier on the limestone floor lit the small chamber with flickering golden light. The lips on the dirt-crusted face parted. "Ahhhhhh."

Her languid posture enraged him further and he charged into the room. "Goddammit, Paloma!" he shouted. "Why did you have to meddle? What does it matter to you if I pay a visit to a human?"

The eyelids of the muddied statue flew open. Black eyes sparkled in the midst of the drying clay. "Have you finally lost your mind, Lowell? I suppose it was inevitable."

He folded his arms over his chest and jutted his chin at her. "Who else would have followed me to Dora's home? Who else would have turned into a bat and made a mess of her sheets? Who else has such contempt for humans?"

Paloma's eyes fell shut and she sighed loudly. "Give me a fucking break, Lowell. I have better things to do than stalk you and interact with some woman's laundry." She curled her lips. "That's just nasty." She lifted her hand from the opaque contents of the pool and tapped its surface, creating plops and splashes in the mud. "Come on in, brother. You sound like you could use a soak."

"Why should I believe you, Paloma? I know about the tricks you play with Calvin. You're a vindictive wench at times."

A mud-flecked Bantam rooster crowed and strutted to the edge of the tub. He tilted his head at Lowell and flapped his wings before rubbing the side of Paloma's dirt-caked head with his beak. "You're pissing off Spare Tyre," she mumbled, eyes still closed. "Just get in here, okay? You'll feel better."

"Fine." Fuming, Lowell undressed and tossed his clothing and boots aside. He sank into the warm mud bath across from his sister. "Ahhh," he breathed. "That's nice." Lowell's head disappeared beneath the surface, then re-emerged, slick as a seal and coated in silt. Lowell wiped the mud from his eyes and rested his shoulders on the side of the pool. "Well, then," he asked, "who do you suppose did it?"

Paloma shrugged. "You're grumpy enough. Who have you aggravated lately?"

"Ach! Still a brat!" Lowell splashed her and laughed. Spare Tyre ruffled his feathers and shifted his weight from foot to foot. Paloma remained still, but Lowell saw the corner of her mouth lift ever-so-slightly as he spoke. "Was it Father, do you suppose? It doesn't seem like something he'd do, but..." His brow furrowed and two brownish-red droplets fell from his beard.

"Beats me," Paloma said. "Seems more likely that it was a rabid bat, but what do I know? At least we can be sure it wasn't the bestest rooster in the whole wide world, right, Spare Tyre?" She smiled and stroked the Bantam's yellow-orange chest with one filthy hand.

Chapter Four

The next morning, Lowell exited Castle Speranza with Dax at his side just as Carmen entered its lawn from the woods. As it had for centuries, the pond behind the structure shone like molten silver, but the addition of flower beds and the newly expanded chicken coop made the castle especially lovely. "Hey, Lowell!" Carmen called. "I've got something for you." She placed a pink and green floral envelope in his hand and winked. "Hope you have a nice day. I'm going to talk with the elves about some grape vines. Don't you think Prescott Vineyards has a nice ring to it?"

She walked away, leaving Lowell alone with his letter and the Labrador they now shared. Lowell darted his eyes from side to side suspiciously and made his way to the clematis-covered pergola in the side yard. Dax, cheerful and unquestioning, followed and sat next to him on the pine bark mulch.

With shaking hands, Lowell tore open the rose-festooned stationery. The page ripped slightly as he withdrew it from the envelope. "Ah, shit," he grumbled, easing it from its wrapping more carefully. He unfolded the page and took a deep breath.

Dear Lowell,

I'm so sorry that the Mathesons interrupted your visit yesterday. They and the Parkers are staying for another night, but I will be done with their breakfasts by ten and free for the rest of the day. All of my guests plan on spending the day in town. Would you like to come to Bohemian Rhapsody once more? I have plans to bake some bread and could use a pair of strong hands to help with the kneading.

Fondly,

Dora Fontaine

Lowell looked up from the page with a racing heart. *She wants me to come back. She thinks of me fondly... And that obnoxious couple in the twin outfits will be nosing around Charade for the day.* He laughed aloud and thumped Dax on his back.

"Care for some refreshment, does he?" a female voice rasped at his elbow. The gnome sniffled and wiped her nose on an orange handkerchief.

"Eh? What's that?" Lowell glanced at the hunched form of the gnome. "Limax? What are you doing here? I thought you worked for Carmen."

Limax sniffled and dabbed her eyes with the cloth. "Oh, I works here and there and all abouts, yes I do, and Carmen's off to talk about squeezing grapes or some such stickiness, anywho. Some apple cider, perhaps, for him? Nicer than the squashy splashes from a grape, I'll wager."

"No, no, nothing at all. I've got things to see and people to do!" Chuckling, Lowell rose and whistled for Dax to come along. "That is..." He laughed. "Ah, you know what I mean, don't you, gnome?"

Limax blew her nose as Lowell strode off through the trees of Prescott Woods.

* * * *

"Hi there," Dora called from inside the house. "My hands are covered in flour, so please just let yourself in, Lowell."

"You be good," Lowell instructed Dax in a low voice. "You can bark if someone shows up, but for goodness's sake, don't make a mess of anything, all right?" Dax sniffed the air then turned once, twice, three times on the rag rug beneath the porch swing. The golden lab rested his head on his paws and closed his eyes.

Lowell entered Bohemian Rhapsody and closed the heavy front door. The mingled scents of vanilla and baking bread greeted him. "Everybody's gone for the day," Dora called from the back of the house. "And when they come back, they know the kitchen's off limits." Lowell made his way past an urn filled with a riot of blooms and beneath the rainbow-tinted glow from the stained glass chandelier.

Dora smiled up at him from behind a massive table decorated with a burning cream-coloured candle. "My guests have stocked mini-fridges, coffee makers and microwaves in their suites, so there's no need for them to come back here anyway. This is part of my private space." Lowell drank in the sight of her—as deliciously full-bodied as a rich brown ale. A dusting of flour decorated the tip of her nose and one cheek, and the frilly ivy-patterned apron exaggerated her hourglass figure. Her small feet, clad in floral sneakers, stood on a white-and-red enamelled step stool.

He placed his hands on the waist of his kilt. "You look very nice, Dora."

"Oh, pooh, I'm covered in flour" — she laughed — "but I'm happy as a pig in mud when I'm baking. Why don't you wash your hands and join me? There's an apron for you next to the sink."

Lowell scrubbed his hands with lemon-infused soap and dried them, then picked up a garment covered in a cheery daisy pattern. He lifted one yellow ribbon strap and curled his lip with disdain. "You don't expect me to...*wear* this, do you?"

"It's my biggest one," she explained. "And there's no one here to see you but me. Don't you want to keep your clothes clean?"

Lowell held up the apron between his fingers and thumbs and raised one eyebrow. A perky green heart decorated the chest panel. "I won't need it." He folded and replaced the apron on the counter. "I'd rather just get dirty."

"Suit yourself." Dora pointed with her chin towards a blue sponge-ware mixing bowl. "You can put a handful of flour on the chopping block and rub it around, then dump that dough on it." Lowell followed her instructions, then stared at the heap of beige matter on the wooden surface. "Now, sprinkle some flour on top and dig the base of your palms into it, like this." Dora demonstrated how to fold, and work the dough. "It's easy, see?"

Lowell watched her flour-covered hands manipulate the mixture before her. It *looked* easy enough. He mimicked her motions carefully. "Yeah, good," she told him. "You'll need to add a little more flour when it gets sticky. We're going to knead it for about fifteen minutes."

The front of Lowell's kilt was already spackled with bits of dough and flour, but he ignored the mess. The dough felt warm and stretchy in his hands.

"We're making beer bread," Dora explained. "The dough recipe called for light rye flour, bread flour, salt and yeast. It's been resting since late yesterday morning."

Lowell grunted, concentrating on his kneading moves. "You serve this to your guests?" he asked.

"Oh, sure," Dora replied. "I'm famous for my breakfasts. Sweet potato casserole, sausage links, parfaits with berries, yogurt and granola and this beer bread." She sprinkled flour on her dough and folded it. "With coffee, tea and fresh orange juice, of course."

A long growl, ending in a curious-sounding high note, emanated from Lowell's abdomen. "Ah, that sounds mighty tasty," he told her.

"I'll fix you a meal after we're done with this," Dora said. "It sounds like you might have skipped breakfast. With that physique, I bet you work up an appetite just breathing, let alone walking all the way here from the woods."

Lowell felt heat rise to his cheeks and bitterly regretted not eating breakfast at the castle.

"Hey, it's okay," Dora said. "Believe me, I get hungry, too. Let's get this dough rising and I'll whip something up. It would give me all kinds of pleasure to fix you a snack. There's nothing more fun than feeding a hungry man." She chuckled and slapped her dough down onto the table. "Well, not much, anyway."

Lowell grunted and the burning sensation in his cheeks lessened. He moved his hands in a smooth kneading rhythm — stretch, fold, turn.

"You're getting the hang of it, you know?" said Dora.

The bright mid-morning light shone through the kitchen window and the soft slap-pat of kneading dough filled the room. Lowell smiled and felt tension in his shoulders ease. The simple motion reminded him of whittling walking sticks from fallen branches during the construction of Castle Speranza.

What a strange time that had been. He had been just a kid, really, although as the oldest, he'd had to take over as a second parent when Mother had died. Father had brought them to a place out of a fairy tale, complete with elves, trolls and fairies, then asked Lowell to watch his siblings as he'd supervised construction of their home. As if the trip from New York to the wilderness of Kentucky hadn't been crazy enough, protecting Paloma, Brock and Korbin from the strange magical folk of the woods had been downright surreal. Lowell had firmly put aside his childhood then and there. With his sister and brothers always in sight, he'd kept a stern expression on his face and tried to be the responsible man his father needed him to be. And whenever possible, he'd done the only thing that had soothed him—picked up a hardwood stick and sliced off one delicate curl of wood at a time. Whisk, slide, turn...whisk, slide, turn...until a pile of shavings lay at his feet and a silky cane slid through his palms.

Funny how pushing around a blob of flour, yeast and beer brought all that back. He could see the appeal of baking, perhaps, but those other inn-related jobs that Dora did were far less enticing.

"You don't mind waiting on people?" he asked. "You don't get tired of cleaning up after their messes and cooking for them?" He shifted on his booted feet.

"I can see why a woman might like flowers and all the frou-frou stuff around here" — he waved a floury hand around in the air — "but the servant part — you actually like that? I mean, washing bedlinens, mopping floors, polishing silver..." He shuddered and thought, *That's what gnomes are for.*

Dora tilted her head from side to side. "Well, I don't suppose I would say that I enjoy the cleaning part, exactly," she answered, "although I do get satisfaction from making my home beautiful. I like gathering sun-dried linens from the clothesline. I love creating satisfying food and serving it in appealing ways." She smiled. "It sounds very old-fashioned, I know, but it pleases me deep-down to present homemade food on lovely china to my guests. Besides, I love my home. Bohemian Rhapsody is filled with the treasures I've collected over the years. Every bit of furniture, every piece of china, all the linens and pillows and rugs — they're all special to me, and it makes them even more valuable when I can show them off." She glanced up at him before looking back down at her hands as they manipulated the dough. "It's hard to explain, Lowell, but running this bed and breakfast makes me very happy." She shrugged. "I could do without the sweeping and mopping and bathroom cleaning, but nothing is perfect in this life, is it?"

Lowell looked across the chopping block at her as she worked. She'd piled her wavy hair atop her head, but a few black curls had escaped to ring her face. The scoop neck of her pink T-shirt was modest, but nothing could hide those curves of hers, he thought. Her cleavage deepened with each shove of her hands into the dough, and he could just detect her heartbeat in the divot above her sternum. She wore a knee-length full skirt that was decorated with cabbage roses ranging in hue from baby pink to magenta to fuchsia. Her expression was peaceful — she was fully absorbed in her task. Lowell stilled his kneading hands as he let his eyes wander over the front of her leaf-festooned smock. Barely veiled by the ruffle of her apron, the sides of her breasts grazed the sides of her upper arms. Through the layers of her bra, T-shirt and apron, he detected the bumps of her erect nipples. Lowell swallowed.

"Don't neglect your dough," Dora scolded. "We've only got a couple more minutes to go, then it will rest for an hour." She glanced at the front of his tan rugby shirt, now smudged with flour. "You should have worn an apron." She let her gaze drop to the front of his kilt, where once more the fabric didn't hang straight down to the floor. Her lips parted and she looked back up at him. Lowell's heart quickened, but he didn't turn away.

"Isn't this stuff done yet?" he asked gruffly. "If it's not ready for a rest, I know that I am."

Dora took out two clean bowls. She coated the dough balls in oil, placed them in the vessels, and covered them with clean kitchen towels. "Okay, they get an hour to rise," she said as she placed them on the counter next to the sink. She started to turn, but Lowell was at her back, holding her in place.

"I enjoyed that, Dora," he whispered in her ear, "but I've got more on my mind than rising bread." He pressed his erection into the small of her back and brushed his lips on the side of her neck. "Am I alone in that? Tell me so, and I'll walk out the door, but..." He exhaled warmth on her skin. "Oh, Dora, I can think of nothing but touching you." He brushed one dark curl from the side of her forehead and ran his fingertip down the side of her face. "Maybe it's wrong, maybe it's too fast, but woman…" He turned her slowly to face him. Light as a feather, Lowell traced the outline of her body from collarbone to the swell of her breast to the gentle curve of her hip. "You make me forget everything," he murmured. Dora took his hand in hers as he spoke. "I feel stupid, ridiculous, bumbling. Should I just go?" She lifted his hand to her lips and kissed one dough-covered knuckle.

Dora shook her head. "You should stay right here."

Chapter Five

Lowell tried to free her hair from the clip that held it, but succeeded only in tangling it further and eliciting a yelp. "Here, let me," she said. He lowered his hands to her waist and watched as she tugged the hinged comb from the bun on top of her head. Seconds later, a rippling cloud of black silk settled around her shoulders.

He took a fistful of her hair, lifted it to his nose and inhaled deeply. "Jasmine?" he murmured.

"Gardenia," Dora corrected. Lowell buried his nose in her hair and placed one roughened hand on her throat. Her heartbeat quickened beneath his palm.

"You are..." he breathed. "Oh, Dora, I don't even know how to put it. I can't think straight around you. You're like..."

"A plus-size Betty Crocker?" she offered.

"A goddess. A goddess from the Old Country, living and breathing in my arms. Venus...Ceres...Diana..." Dora untied her apron and tossed it aside, then pulled her T-shirt over her head. Lowell's jaw dropped. "You are Persephone," he breathed. "She of the golden apples."

"Triple Ds," Dora informed him. "All natural." She lifted his hand and placed it over one lace-covered breast.

He stroked the pad of his thumb over her stiffened nipple, rosy pink beneath a sheer swath of dove grey lace. "The brassiere is beautiful," he said haltingly, "but perhaps...if you don't mind..."

Dora reached behind her back and unhooked the bra. A stricken sound came from Lowell's throat as she slid the pale garment off and set it aside. His jaw worked, but no words came from his mouth. She took his hands in hers and placed one on each heavy tit. "You can touch them, Lowell. I'd like for you to."

He caught her eye briefly, and seeing his own excitement mirrored in her face, he hefted her breasts in his hands and licked his lips. "No guests are coming?" he murmured. "No more retirees in matching warm-up suits?"

"Not until later today," Dora answered. "And, even then, I don't need to bother with them." She walked to the kitchen door and locked it with a sliding bolt, then turned back to him. Her breasts, each crowned by a hardened peak, hung heavy and soft above her narrow waist and wide hips. Her skirt swished about her thighs as she walked back to him. "I have an idea, Lowell." A sly smile curled her lips. "If you really don't mind getting dirty, that is."

"With you?" He chuckled. "Never."

She picked up a small piece of glazed crockery. "This is a French butter dish." She took off the top of the crock to reveal a bowl filled with a pale yellow substance. "It keeps butter fresh and at room temperature, so it's easy to spread." Lowell cocked one eyebrow at her. "You're awfully good at kneading," Dora whispered. "You're a natural. I was starting to get jealous of the dough..." She offered the butter dish to him, then sat on the middle rung of her step chair next to the chopping block. With a practiced hand, she tugged the fold-out steps from beneath it to serve as a footrest.

Lowell chuckled and shook his head. "I'd be a boor to let you feel ignored," he said, "especially since I've much more affection for these lovelies of yours than I do for a bit of beer and flour." He scooped an ample amount of butter from the dish and rubbed his palms to coat them. "Slippery." Dora's eyes fell shut when his buttered hands met her body. Lowell spread the stuff over her skin, taking extra time to play with the greased nubs of her nipples. Humming to himself, he slipped his fingers in the folds beneath her breasts and massaged her skin reverently. "So warm," he murmured, "and so silky."

Dora arched her back and sighed, then reached behind her on the chopping block. Lowell watched, spellbound, as she held a glass jar with a metal cap at neck level. She tipped the jar and sprinkled a sparkly brown powder on each thickened nipple. "Try it." She rolled her shoulders so that her breasts moved enticingly before his mouth. "It's sweet."

Lowell felt hypnotised. "Oh, woman," he growled. "You're a temptress of the best sort." He cupped one full breast in his hands so that the spice-dusted nipple pointed up to his lips, then looked up at Dora. She nodded, eyes glimmering with excitement, and leaned towards him. He bent over and gave her breast an experimental lick, then, groaning, pulled the stiff peak into his mouth. Dora exhaled and brought her fingers to his head, tugging him closer to her chest. Lowell curled his tongue around her nipple, swallowed and sucked harder.

He grunted in surprise when Dora found his erection with her hands, then let her breast slide from his mouth. "Mmm," Lowell growled, "that's what it ought to look like. Plump and shiny-wet from a man's mouth." He raised her other breast and drew it between his lips.

Dora giggled and squirmed. "Your whiskers just tickle a bit," she said in explanation, "but it's okay." She kept her left hand on his shaft and took her right breast in her free hand, running the hardened peak down the side of his face, over his cheekbone to the top of his beard. Lowell's eyes dropped shut and he swallowed, salivating. Dora tickled his lips with her right nipple. "Suck on both of them," she whispered. "Please."

Lowell grunted and opened his mouth. Her nipple popped free at once. Dora pressed her breasts together with both hands so that the ruddy peaks touched each other. "Try it, Lowell." Groaning, he drew both nipples between his lips. "You'll have to suck hard," Dora instructed, "so they stay in your mouth." She scooted to the edge of the seat and raised her skirt to her hips. "I'm so wet," she murmured. "You just keep doing what you're doing, okay? Don't worry about being too rough." Lowell felt one of her hands wrap around his erection and detected movement between her legs from the other. "I like having your mouth on me." She squirmed on the seat and pumped his length in her hand.

Lowell, with the flavours of butter, cinnamon and sugar lingering in his mouth, nibbled and pulled harder as her gasps grew louder. "That's good," Dora breathed. "Oh, swallow me, suck me, don't stop..."

Her body tensed and she squeezed his erection, crying out in a throaty yell.

Lowell remained still until she quieted, then let his mouth fall open. Reddened, slick and swollen, her peaks fell back to their natural positions. "Hot damn, Lowell Rossi," Dora smiled. "That was fantastic." She grabbed the waistband of his kilt, unbuckled it and cast it aside. "What are we going to do about this thing, though?" She gripped his shaft in both hands and pulled him closer.

"You've made me all slick," she whispered. "All sensitive and slippery." Dora flicked the head of his cock against one stiff nipple. Lowell placed his hands on her shoulders to steady himself. He watched as she rubbed his erection against her breasts, playing with each hardened peak. A trace of sugared grittiness remained on her breasts, but the thick coating of butter kept it from chafing his skin. A clear drop of pre-cum shone on the taut tip of his shaft. Dora exhaled and lifted one breast to coat her nipple with the shining stuff. Lowell squeezed her shoulders and worked his jaw silently.

"I wonder..." Dora said quietly. She pressed her breasts together around his erection with one hand and forearm and gripped his rear with the other. "What would it feel like if you moved it in and out right here?"

Lowell growled and bucked his hips. Once the motion was begun, it became unstoppable. He watched the rosy head of his cock peek from the crevice of her breasts, then hide again as it slid beneath them. Dora glanced up at him and caught her lower lip between her teeth. "Looks delicious," she murmured. "It's making me hungry." Lowell grunted and pumped faster. He lifted one hand to Dora's cheek, and she turned her face to draw his first finger between her lips. She sucked it past her teeth, scraping lightly, until she nibbled the rounded knuckle at the finger's base. She swallowed and let the wet digit slide back out.

"I want it," Dora whispered.

Lowell closed his eyes as tingling heat grew in his groin. Breathing faster, he found her nipples with his fingers and pinched them as he fucked her cleavage.

"I want it in my mouth." Lowell froze. Dora, her hand still wrapped around his shaft, scooted down one rung of the step-stool. She stuck out her tongue and licked the head of his cock experimentally, then looked up at him. Lowell wove his fingers into her hair and thrust his pelvis, brushing his engorged tip against her chin.

Dora ran her hands over his bare rear. "It's been so long since a man's come in my mouth," she said. She sucked the knob of his erection and squeezed the spots where his upper thighs met his ass. Lowell's shaft twitched. "I'd like it, wouldn't you?" He gripped her hair tighter and watched his cock disappear between her lips.

"Ohhhh, woman," he moaned. "Dora, Dora, Dora..."

She said nothing but, swallowing, moved her head faster. Her breasts bumped against his thighs and Lowell felt the occasional delicate strafe of her nipples on his skin. He tensed and placed his hands behind her on the heavy chopping block. "I don't want to hurt you," he forced out. "I don't want to push too deep." He braced himself on the wooden surface and ground his jaw so hard that his teeth squeaked.

Dora let his erection slide free. She took the base of his shaft in both hands and licked his tip, then replaced one hand on the curve of his ass. "I want it all, Lowell," she stated. She pulled his face down to hers and kissed him, pushing her tongue between his lips and pumping her fist over his cock. Lowell felt the surge of his orgasm begin.

"I want it down my throat."

He bellowed when she lowered her face and sucked his length over her tongue. She held it there, swallowing around his girth, and squeezed and pumped the base of his erection with her fist.

"I'm coming... Right now... If you're sure—" He bucked his hips as his climax hit. Gulping, Dora tugged him closer and held him until the last trembling spasms subsided.

"By a troll's melon-sized balls," he breathed. "I've never come so hard." Lowell stroked one hand fondly over Dora's dark hair, then tensed in alarm. "Oh, forgive my crudeness, madam."

Dora let his softening erection fall from her mouth. She wiped her lips with her fingertips and the trace of a smile curled on her lips. "You can be crude if you like," she chuckled. "You just came in my mouth, you know."

Lowell looked away, embarrassed.

"And I'm so very glad you did," she added. Dora stood and wrapped her arms around him, pressing her gritty-slick breasts against his bare chest. He felt the curve of her cheek on his neck as she continued. "I've never had so much fun baking bread. It's been simply—" She froze and her head snapped up. "What in the hell is that? An armadillo?" Lowell spun about and caught a glimpse of movement through the kitchen window.

Dora bolted away, grabbed her T-shirt and yanked it on as she flew out the door. "Shoo, shoo!" she yelled. "Go on, git!"

Lowell slapped his kilt around his hips and chased after her. All he saw was the flapping hem of her skirt and one sneakered heel disappear around the corner of her house. When he caught up with her in the front yard, she had her fists on her hips and a dazed expression on her face. "Damnedest thing," she muttered. "An armadillo in Charade! Bold thing too, and it sure could run..."

She shook her head and trotted back to her backyard. "Just look at my peonies!" she moaned. "What in the world would possess an armadillo to dig up my peonies?" The plants' roots were bare and neat piles of soil flanked the plants like a row of attentive, muddy soldiers. Her brow furrowed. She picked up a sodden plant with dangling roots and one dainty violet bloom. "That crazy thing dragged a columbine over here!" she said, incredulous. "I wonder if it was rabid?"

Lowell stormed back into her house to fetch his shirt, boots and socks. He emerged, seething, as Dax loped up. "And just where were you this whole time?" He shot an icy glance at the golden lab. "Some guard dog you are."

Dora shrugged and patted Dax's blond head. "Oh well, no harm done. Want to help me get them replanted, Lowell? I suppose I'll find a place for this columbine while I'm at it, if it can survive being dragged around by a disease-ridden armadillo."

Fury surged through Lowell's face and ran down to his clenched fists. "I've got something to take care of," he grumbled. "I'll have to take a rain check, Dora. Thank you for the...ah..." His cheeks warmed once more and he tugged his beard self-consciously. "Well, I'm off then." He stalked off like a shot with Dax by his side.

Chapter Six

"You're the last one I'd have expected this from, Korbin." Lowell strode into the Castle Speranza library and directed his ire at his fair-haired youngest brother. "But I suppose that's why you've been getting away with it. I never knew you had such a sick sense of humour."

"Huh?" Korbin looked up from a massive tome, blinking owlishly. "Humour? Me? Never." He shook his head dismissively and looked back down at the printed pages before him. "Nope, no idea what you're going on about," he murmured.

"Sure you don't." Lowell paced around the heavy table with his arms crossed. "Look at you, all innocent and bookish, all immersed in your research." He slammed the book shut with a noisy thump. "But you've been stalking about, ruining Dora's laundry and digging up her plants, haven't you? Putting on glamours of bats and armadillos, just for kicks? Trying to scare her away from me out of pathetic jealousy, hmm?" Lowell lowered his face to Korbin's until their noses almost touched. "Back off, little brother, or I'll make you regret the day you were born."

Korbin rose to his feet, white-blond hair flying. "You're the one who needs to back off, Lowell!" he retorted. "I'm sick of your threats and nonsense. Of course I haven't been bothering Dora. It doesn't seem like anything I'd do" — he scowled and braced his fists on his hips — "because I'd never even consider it." He gestured towards the leather-bound books spread across the library table. "I've got far too many more important things on my plate than to worry about your love life. Give me a break."

"What's all this? Reading up on cheesecake, Lowell?" Brock entered the room, sat in one of the leather armchairs and propped up his feet. "I can't get Dora's dessert out of my mind, either, to tell you the truth." He smacked his lips and patted his stomach with a chuckle.

"Aarrrgh, it's you, isn't it?" Lowell snarled. He moved behind Brock and yanked the chair away from the table. "Damn you and your foolishness!" Lowell, bellowing in fury, picked up the chair with Brock in it and lifted it off the floor. "I should throw you across the room!" Grunting with effort and rage, he shook the chair and growled. The chandelier overhead trembled.

"Hey, now!" Brock soothed, knuckles whitening around the arms of his chair. "I know we're all immortal here, but that doesn't mean that getting squashed wouldn't sting a little." Lowell bared his teeth. "And no, Lowell, I haven't been doing anything foolish lately, at least around you, so you can relax." Korbin, moving slowly, put his hands on the arms of Brock's uplifted chair and, catching Lowell's eye, eased it to the floor.

Lowell grunted and scrubbed his hands through his hair. "Surely not Father," he murmured in a daze. "Father would never debase himself in such a fashion…or would he?"

"What's this?" Gavin Rossi boomed from the doorway. "What sort of debasement are you wondering if I'm capable of?"

"Ah," Lowell began. "That is, um, you'd never… Uh…"

"Put on glamours and skulk about Lowell and his ladylove," offered Korbin. "Mess about in a human's laundry and shrubbery."

"And generally be foolish, just to get under Lowell's skin," Brock added helpfully. "Was that pretty much it, Lowell?"

Gavin looked from Brock's mirth-filled face to Korbin's irritated one, then turned to his oldest son. Silently, he shook his head, then left the room.

"Was that a 'No', I take it?" Brock quipped.

Lowell growled and grabbed the back of Brock's chair once more. In a swift motion, he tipped it backwards until the back rested on the floor and Brock's surprised face stared up at the ceiling. "Birdbrain," Lowell grumbled. "Why don't you go play with the damn chickens?"

"Any of these ones wanting for refreshies?" Mephita stood, knobby hands akimbo and gangly knees stretching down from her homespun tunic. "Tea, cider?" She leaned in to the library and grinned. "And, oh yes, eggsies cooked up devilish-style. Carmen instructored this old Mephita 'bout how Miss Dora makes them." She chuckled. "That one's a good cook, yes, and he knows it, true?" She leered at Lowell, displaying the herbal remnants of her last meal in the gaps between her teeth.

"Out of my way, gnome," muttered Lowell. Mephita shrank away as he stalked from the room, chased by Brock's and Korbin's guffaws.

* * * *

Boom-boom-boom — and the sweet lilt of the oboe fluttered up over the percussion.

"Figure eights," instructed Carmen. "No hurry, let's just try to get them slow and perfect, ladies." Dora checked out her classmates to her right and left. Beth, Deb, Colby and Bernice, attired in stretchy leggings, hip scarves and tank tops, wore matching expressions of deep concentration. Dora, however, felt nothing but blissful, easy relaxation as she rolled her hips through the motions.

"Really, Dora, you don't have to make it look so easy," Bernice complained. "Not all of us were born with hips that will just naturally swish around like this." The slim, silver-tressed librarian scowled.

"Shhh, Bernice, Dora can't help it if her hips do all the work for her," said Carmen. "And you're doing great! Just relax and enjoy and don't worry about what anybody else is doing."

Bernice grunted and turned her back to Dora, then resumed her hip rolls.

Colby flipped her platinum bob and looked thoughtful. "You know, Dora, I haven't seen you look so, um, relaxed in quite a while." Dora shrugged as warmth rose to her cheeks, but kept silent. "It's almost as if there were some romance going on in your life." Dora smiled and kept her eyes fixed forward.

"She got a haircut and deep conditioning treatment yesterday," tattled Beth. "She hadn't passed through the doors of Hippie Chic for at least six months, but she'd called a few days ago and said she needed me to get her in as soon as possible. She even got a bikini wax, you guys, and I saw her going in to the nail salon right after. Clearly she's getting gussied up for somebody, right? So who's the lucky man, Dora? Did one of your B&B guests get a little more than a free breakfast with his last stay?"

Dora cleared her throat. "I would never mix business and pleasure, Beth. That is totally unprofessional."

"Yeah, and it might screw up her TripAdvisor ratings," Bernice noted.

Deb giggled. "Or send them soaring through the roof..."

"Ladies!" scolded Carmen. "If Dora wants to keep her new romance a secret from us, even though we are her best friends and would never tell anyone, that's her choice. Let's move on to some vertical hip circles and head slides. Concentrate on precision."

For a few minutes, conversation ceased in the gazebo behind Prescott Manor as the six women shimmied, rolled and stepped in the balmy spring air. A dewy layer of sweat covered each woman's stomach and back as she danced, and the plaintively beautiful Middle Eastern music wended through the gardens. Dora was grateful for the halt to the barrage of questions, but it turned out to be only a temporary respite.

"Out with it, Dora!" Bernice ordered. "Small town like this, we gotta get our kicks where we can, and there's nothing more thrilling than dating somebody new."

"Well..." Dora admitted. "I have been on a few dates with someone special."

Carmen raised an eyebrow and caught Dora's eye. "Someone on the manly side?"

"Oh, yes, he's definitely manly," Dora giggled. "In more ways than one."

"Hot damn! Did you take any pictures?" asked Bernice. "Oooh, or video? Got it on YouTube yet?"

"Sorry, Bernice, no images to share. He's...kind of old-fashioned and a little silly at times, but he seems quite fond of me." She slid her head from side to side as she spoke. "A bit self-conscious, but it's actually endearing in a funny way."

"Go on," Deb urged. Her carrot-red curls glowed in the afternoon sun. "As an old married woman, I need to be reminded of how fun dating is. Marcus thinks that the same old incense and massage oil will do the trick every time."

"What're you complaining about? I'd love to have a man light some incense and rub on me. Send that husband of yours right over!" Bernice cackled.

"Well, it's not all perfect," conceded Dora. "He just gets so flustered and upset that he sort of ruins it every now and then, but then he comes back and he's just so cute and charming..." She bit her lower lip, remembering, as the music dwindled to a close. "Sometimes bumbling and tripping over his words when he talks, but then he stops talking and, well, there's nothing awkward about his body, girls."

"Mm-hm," Carmen sighed. "Anybody thirsty besides me? I've got some peach iced tea. Be right back."

Bernice turned to Dora. "What's this bumbling manly man getting upset about?" she asked. "Does he lose his temper?"

"Oh, no, never at me. He just gets mad when, like, something goes wrong, and he'll blush and fuss and go stomping off."

"What in the world's been going wrong?" wondered Colby. "Creepy guests at the inn?"

"No, the guests at Bohemian Rhapsody are fine — the human sort that is. It's the animals that are causing trouble. You know, when one of those armadillos that are on the prowl digs into my garden, or a rat knocks over the bin of fertiliser, or a bat gets into the laundry." She chuckled. "I thought his head was going to explode the other day when we got home from a walk and a buzzard had knocked over some of my potted plants, and then there was that turtle..."

"Prowling buzzards and bats in broad daylight?" asked Deb. "Sorry for asking, Dora, but were you the only one to see these creatures?" She lifted her pinched index finger and thumb to her pursed lips, inhaled deeply and crossed her eyes.

Dora punched Deb lightly on the bicep. "Nothing like that, you old hippie, but yes, I'm the only one who's seen them, and that seems to make him even madder. I don't know what he thinks he would do with a rat or a buzzard if he caught it, but it kills him that they're getting away. Every time something's gotten messed with, he gets bent out of shape that he hasn't laid eyes on the perpetrator and then goes off in a huff."

"What in the hell is going on at your place? Armadillos, bats, turtles, rats... Are you starting a damn zoo over there? Bed, breakfast and petting farm?" Bernice chortled. "Don't think that many kiddos are gonna be interested in petting buzzards, though, Dora, I hate to break it to you."

"The animals have been going a bit nuts around my place," Dora sighed, "but what can I do? I'm just chalking it up to spring fever. I guess I've been too distracted with this" — she smiled — "little romance of mine that I haven't had time to care about the critters. A mess or two isn't going to spoil my fun."

The side door swung shut and Carmen strode towards the gathering with a tray full of tumblers and a pitcher of tea.

"Well?" Bernice asked. She distributed glasses of amber tea as Carmen filled them.

"Huh?" asked Dora.

"His *name*," Colby prodded.

"Who is it?" Deb asked insistently.

"Oh, his name." Dora twitched her hips, raised her arms to shoulder-height and rolled her ribs. "Lowell Rossi," she breathed. "His name is Lowell."

Dora caught a glimpse of the mottled brown skin of a hognose snake as it parted the iris leaves and slid out of view between the roses.

Chapter Seven

"Lowell, thank you for another lovely afternoon. I never knew you were such an expert at rowing a canoe. I felt like one of those women in old photographs, being squired about by her beau. You were tireless today, just like you are when you do certain other things for me in the Queen Anne's Lace room." Dora cupped her hand around the bulge in his crotch. "Speaking of, would you care to come back with me to my bedroom? I just put some new sheets on the bed and I'd love to" — she squeezed lightly — "break them in."

Lowell glanced at the red-orange glow on the skyline. "I'm going to have to be going before too long, my dear, but I suppose I've got a few minutes to... Ah..." He groaned as Dora slipped one hand up the hem of his kilt and found his erection. "Let's go check out the thread count," he growled.

He scooped her into his arms and thumped down the hallway to her bedroom. "You smell gorgeous, woman. What is that scent — rose?"

Dora traced her fingers down the side of his face and raked her nails through his beard. "Nuh-uh," she corrected. "It's orange blossom."

He strode into her room and tossed her on the bed, where her body sank into the puffy loft of her down mattress topper. Dora giggled. "But I don't care if you know what I smell like, lover, as long as it turns you on."

"Aye," Lowell nodded, eyes glimmering. He pulled his T-shirt over his head and chuckled. "That it does, that it does."

Dora beckoned him closer to the side of the bed. "C'mere, I haven't admired that chest of yours lately." She spread her hands over his expanse of rippled muscle and flat belly, then pressed her face to his stomach. In between kisses, she whispered, "I love the little tufts of hair right here...and the curve of your muscle right here...and the ridges over your abdomen...and your sweet little belly button...and I especially love this part that's under it..." She fumbled with the buckle of his kilt, then let the garment drop to the floor.

"Oh, yes, there it is." Dora gripped his erection in both hands. "Have a seat, Mr Rossi. I have a little present for you." Lowell scooted back onto the bed, cock pointing up at attention.

She opened her bedside table and drew out a white and black box. "Look what I bought at Stoner's Drug Emporium," she said. "These are the biggest ones they had, for men of maximum length and girth." Dora drew her lower lip between her teeth and stepped between his knees. "I hope I'm not being presumptuous, but you've been on my mind a lot" — she touched the head of his shaft with her fingertip — "and, well, we haven't, you know, done everything there is to do together, and I've been thinking that perhaps it was time…"

Lowell picked her up and placed her in the middle of the mattress. "You're a brilliant woman, Dora," he said. "I love the way your mind works." He tugged off her sneakers and socks and tossed them to the floor, then set to work on her sundress.

"You can just slip it over my head," Dora told him.

"Shush. Can't you see I'm busy here?" Button by button, he opened her dress down the front, exposing her deep cleavage, soft stomach and lacy panties. He slipped the dress from her arms, hardened cock bumping against her legs as he worked, then reached behind her to unfasten her brassiere. A deep growl emanated from his throat as her breasts fell free — Lowell placed one wet kiss on each thickened nipple. "Now these," he muttered, "have got to go." He slid her panties down over her hips and threw them over his shoulder.

Dora chewed on her thumb as he tore open the box and withdrew a crinkling square of plastic. "Extra-large, huh?" he muttered. "Might be big enough, I suppose."

She plucked at the cotton cover on the down mattress. "Given what I've felt with my, you know, mouth, and the fact that it's been a little while since I've welcomed a man to my bed…"

"You're thinking it'll be a bit of a stretch, are you?"

Dora pressed her lips together and nodded. "Okay, yes, and I'm a little nervous."

"Hmm, then, we can't have that," Lowell noted. "Why don't you rest your pretty head on the pillow and think happy thoughts, and I'll see what I can do."

Dora fell back and exhaled slowly. "When it's just you and me, with no distractions, it's pretty amazing, don't you think, Lowell?" She stretched her arms over her head and searched for words. "It's like we're wrapped in a little cocoon that we've made, growing into something beautiful together." Lowell kissed the inside of each of her knees. "Sometimes change hurts a bit, though, you know? Growing pains and all."

"I'll be gentle, don't you worry, my poetic lady," he assured her. "We'll turn into butterflies or moths or whatever winged bugs you have in mind, and you won't feel anything but good. I'd never let anything hurt you, I promise."

Dora felt the bristles of his beard scrape her inner thigh and squirmed, giggling. "Shhh…" he insisted. "Be still." He planted kisses up one thigh, stopping at the juncture of her legs, then started at the other knee and worked his way to her centre. Dora willed her trembling, ticklish muscles to stop moving and took a deep breath.

She cried out when his lips met the rumpled folds between her legs. He licked her skin slowly, unfurling her lower lips with the tip of his tongue. Dora combed his dark hair with her fingers as he kissed her, then gasped when he sucked the edge of her labia into his mouth and tugged. Lowell chuckled. "Feeling a bit more at ease?" he asked.

Dora hummed in response and tilted her hips towards his face. He found the nub of her clit with his tongue and eased two roughened fingers into her sheath. "Oh, yes," Dora breathed.

Even though his fingers filled her, Dora began to yearn for something thicker inside her. She placed both her hands on his head and urged him to come up from between her legs. "I'm ready," she whispered. He kissed her inner thigh—she felt the dampness left by his beard on her skin—and knelt between her legs.

A tremor of excited nervousness fluttered in her stomach. He tore open the foil pouch and unrolled the condom on his shaft—his very *thick* shaft.

"Tight fit," he muttered, "but it'll do."

Dora's heart raced as he settled on top of her. His body was bulky and massive—with his black chest hair and beard, he looked like an enormous Roman warrior. Maybe he *was* Zeus visiting in human form...

"Lowell?" she asked in quiet voice.

"Mmmm." He gripped his erection and nudged it at her opening.

"You're, like, a regular person, right? You're not going to make love to me and then turn me into a swan or a cow or something with magical powers, are you?"

Lowell caught her eye and Dora saw something inscrutable pass over his face. "I, ah, promise not to turn you into any animals."

She cried out when he eased the head of his cock inside her. "Slowly!" she said.

Lowell paused, just the tip of his shaft in her body, and found her breast with his mouth. Her nipple puckered on his tongue. Ripples of heat ran from her cunt outward, sending delicious shivers to her belly, her breasts, her mouth and even her toes. A warm sensation grew in her core and she thrust her hips against his. "Better," she breathed as he eased deeper inside.

He released her breast and cupped her face in his broad hand. "Much better," he growled.

Dora felt that she was in the midst of a heady war of sensations—a cloud of down beneath her back, a hardened muscle-bound man atop her, an oh-my-God tight stretch in her cunt and—most blissful of all—his adoring eyes looking down at her. Liquid, black and adoring, they promised everything, and his lips reinforced it without a word. He kissed her tenderly, touching his lips to hers with the sweetest of pressures, then pushed his tongue into her mouth, just as he slid his cock farther within her…

Dora whimpered and gripped his rear urgently. "Best," she groaned. "Do it, Lowell, All the way." He fucked her faster, stretching her with each stroke. She wrapped her legs around his upper thighs and panted. "Yeah… That's good."

"I'm not hurting you?" he asked in a strained voice.

"Nuh-uh. Don't hold back." Dora scraped her fingernails down his back and squeezed her inner muscles around his shaft.

Lowell slammed into her. The antique bed creaked and thumped against the wall—Dora wondered briefly if the guests had returned and were overhearing, then all rational thought escaped from her mind. There was just this man, this glorious man on top of her and inside her, pushing deeper with every stroke, and her own body, shuddering and on fire beneath him.

"There." She squeezed her eyes closed. "There!" she shouted. "I'm coming, Lowell—don't stop!" He bellowed, pumping faster, as she stiffened beneath him. The bed spun and the room tilted and every nerve in her body caught fire. Lowell slammed into her with all his might once, twice and the third time Dora felt a surge of energy leave his body and enter hers. He sank on top of her, breathing raggedly, and Dora cupped his rear as the last trembling spasms were spent.

Then she heard a tremendous crash from the direction of the kitchen.

"What in the world?" She rolled Lowell to the side of the mattress, slipped off the bed in a flash and scurried down the hall.

"Wait, wait!" Lowell bellowed, thundering after her.

"I'll be damned," Dora muttered. She raised her hand to the mess and then let it drop, limp, to her side. "What would possess a toad to get into my kitchen and knock over the flour and salt?"

"A toad?" roared Lowell. "Where is the damned thing? Show it to me and I'll squash it like a grape."

"Ugh, don't be gruesome." Dora shuddered. "I suppose I need to lock up the house more tightly. It must have hopped in through the window."

"Enough is enough!" yelled Lowell. He marched to the back door and threw it open. "You leave us the hell alone!" he thundered. "I don't know who you are or what your game is, but I swear by all that is holy that I'll make you sorry for the day you tangled with Lowell Rossi!" The backyard was silent and peaceful in the pre-twilight gloaming. A swallowtail butterfly floated in front of Lowell's face. He swatted it down to the grass with a growl and raised his fist to the sky. "Dammit, I'll not take it anymore!"

"I beg your pardon, Lowell, but this is my house and my garden, and that was my butterfly you just mangled." Dora grabbed his elbow and whipped him around to face her. "Perhaps you haven't noticed, but it's my stuff—my food, my plants, my trash, my laundry—that's getting ruined around here, and I'm the one who has to deal with it. You fuss and carry on as if you're the one offended, and then you run off and leave me to tidy the mess." She widened her eyes and raised her voice. "They're just dumb animals, Lowell! Screaming at them to be good isn't going to do a single thing, but helping me clean up would certainly be appreciated."

Lowell, breathing hard, ground his jaw and clenched his fists. "You don't understand what's going on here, Dora, and I" — he shook his head — "I just can't tell you everything right now. I'm trying to do everything right with you but someone..." He ground his jaw in annoyance. "Someone is making it very difficult for me."

He stormed out of the back door, called for Dax, and disappeared from sight. Dora looked around at the powdery white mess on her kitchen surfaces and floor. "Wouldn't kill you to help me out, would it, Mr Rossi?" she complained.

Shaking her head, she dampened a couple of paper towels and approached the table first. "Dumb lug," she grumbled. "Too handsome and too silly for your own good." She spread the white stuff out on the wooden plane and licked one finger. She drew a plus sign in the flour, with the letters D and F on the top two sections and L and R on the bottom, then enclosed the whole thing in a curvy heart. "See there, Lowell, how nice that looks?" she whispered and added a diagonal arrow through the heart. "It could be just lovely, Mr Rossi."

She stared at her powdery handiwork for a moment, then swept the paper towels over the letters, scooped up a dusty pile and dumped it into the waste bin. "But first, you've got to learn to roll with the punches, Lowell." Dora lifted the plastic garbage can to the edge of the table and brushed the salt and flour mixture into it with determined strokes. "You're great at getting me hot, but you've got to hang with me during the tough times if you want to keep this fire burning."

* * * *

"Lowell, I understand your anger, I do." Calvin Prescott popped the top off another frosted bottle of Sam Adams and rejoined his guest in the den of Prescott Manor. "But you seem to have forgotten that I am not one of the Fair Folk. There's not a drop of magic in me, and I certainly don't cast glamours." He took a swallow of his own beer before continuing. "Moreover, I'm the last one to stand between you and Dora. Thanks to your sister..." He sighed. "I've come to learn that true love is the most valuable thing in this life, although it's too late for me to do anything about it now." He ran one liver-spotted hand over his balding scalp. "Besides, I'm fond of Dora Fontaine. I'd never want to cause her any trouble."

"Of course I know you're not one of the Fair Folk," Lowell grumbled, "but I thought you might know something about what's been happening. I'm at my wits' end, I don't mind saying. This madness has been going on for weeks now." He glared at the grandfather clock — its ceaseless tick-ticking was infuriating. Lowell wanted to yank the pendulum off the thing, smash the clock's face then tip it over onto the floor. Sure, it would be violent and destructive, but the elves could fix it all up tomorrow... He balled his hands into fists and curled his lips wickedly.

"I do wish I could help, but I'm afraid that I know nothing about it." Calvin's brows drew together and he stood. "I've had some frustrations of my own, you know, of the gardening variety."

Lowell turned to him with a snap. "Somebody digging up your plants?" he asked sharply. "Knocking over your flowerpots? Spilling your fertiliser?"

"Oh, no, nothing like that." Calvin shook his head. "Poor Dora's got the worse end of things, I'm afraid. The hooligans have left Prescott Manor alone, but…" He strode to the wide window that faced the woods and looked down at the moonlit gardens. "Maybe it's hard to see in this light, but my gardens have been neglected a bit lately." He laughed uncomfortably. "I didn't want to say anything to your family, because, after all, it's free labour from the gnomes, trolls and elves that made the manor and its gardens a reality. I don't want to appear ungrateful. It's just…"

Lowell rose and stood next to Calvin.

"Well, see there?" Calvin pointed. "That rose plant is covered in spent blooms, and there are a few dandelions in the irises. The wisteria is starting to look a little shaggy, too."

Lowell grunted.

"I know, I know," Calvin murmured. "It's a bit silly. I'm just spoilt on an immaculate garden. It's just that it's so *unlike* Bufo to miss things like that."

"Maybe we're being too easy on them," grumbled Lowell. "After that business with Mephita and Brock, damn gnomes think they have the run of the place. Using our family bathing cavern, sneaking about and eavesdropping, getting more underfoot and wilful day by day."

"Now, now, I don't want to cause a fuss." Calvin turned from the window and sank back down into the leather sofa. "It's springtime, after all, and it's hard to keep up with all the growth in the gardens. The plants and animals both are a little wild this time of year. Maybe it's the season of love for gnomes as well — who knows?" He propped his slippered feet up on the coffee table. "And that's probably all that's been happening at Bohemian Rhapsody, you know. A concentration of animals getting into trouble in the same place. Stranger things have happened."

Lowell took a swig of his beer and stared out the window at the gardens, still spectacular in their quasi-neglected state, and at the depths of the woods beyond. *Perhaps,* he thought. *Perhaps.*

He rejoined Calvin on the couch. "Many thanks, Calvin, for your hospitality, and I'll take the gardening issues up with Bufo" —he rolled his eyes— "*gently.*" He drew a deep breath. "There's something else I want to talk about with you. Something that would mean quite a bit of change, I'm afraid."

"Yes?" Calvin prodded. "Go on. I'm intrigued."

"Well, it's about the manor. You do have quite a lot of room here for just one person…"

Chapter Eight

Dora propped herself up on one elbow and looked out of the open window. The sheer lacy curtain billowed in the afternoon breeze, carrying the scent of roses and kitchen herbs into her bedroom. She closed her eyes and breathed deeply. Her new sateen sheets were cool and silky on her bare skin, and the birdsong that sparkled through the air was lovelier than any symphony. "Hear that?" she whispered. "Wood thrush. Henry David Thoreau said, 'Whenever a man hears it he is young, and Nature is in her spring; whenever he hears it, it is a new world and a free country, and the gates of Heaven are not shut against him'."

Lowell slid his roughened hands over her bare side. "My Danae," he murmured. "Even Zeus could never stay away from you, my sweet." He cupped one bare breast in his hand and smiled. "Who cares about a silly bird when I have you naked in my bed?"

Dora laughed lightly. "You mean *my* bed," she corrected. "My bed, my house, my garden. We've made love everywhere there is to do it, Lowell, except at your place." She spread her fingers over his chest and fluffed his dark chest hair. "Not that I'm complaining. Well, not exactly." She traced the lines of his pectorals. "But it would be kind of nice to see where you live. In a little cabin in the woods, like Hansel and Gretel? Do you have a lab for your biology studies?"

Lowell swallowed and cleared his throat. "Sort of," he mumbled. "But I want to talk to you about something, Dora, now that we're on the topic of houses. It's a bit radical, but it would allow us to see more of each other and perhaps, um, grow even closer."

"Pray tell." Dora rolled onto her stomach to look at him.

"Well, ah." His face coloured. "You know how I feel about you…"

"Like I'm a hot human princess and you're a sex-crazed immortal?" offered Dora.

Lowell's chuckles dissolved into a coughing fit. He sat up as Dora thumped him on the back, then settled back onto the mattress. "Okay, here goes." He took one of her hands between his work-worn ones. "You could move into Prescott Manor, Dora. You could run your bed and breakfast there. There's plenty of room—Calvin has his own wing, there's a wing just for you, and the six guest suites run down the middle of the house. You'd even have your own kitchen, separate from Calvin's, on your side of the manor."

Dora, baffled, scanned his face and pulled her hand away. "Why in the world would I want to do that?" she asked. "I love Bohemian Rhapsody. It may not be Prescott Manor, all fine and fancy, but I happen to like my little B&B. I certainly don't want to move in with Calvin Prescott—I hardly know him!—and I can't imagine that he wants me to. Have you lost your mind completely, Lowell Rossi?"

"No, no, I haven't, just listen!" Lowell insisted. "You wouldn't have to clean the house any more, or even garden when you didn't want to. Calvin has his own team of gardeners, repairmen and cleaners. I know there are things you'd like to improve on at Bohemian Rhapsody, things you'd like to fix. If you moved to Prescott Manor, you could just focus on what you love — cooking and entertaining — and let the staff take care of the repairs and drudge work." He took her hand once more and kissed her palm. "And you'd be closer to where I live." He paused and continued in a whisper. "Maybe you'd even want to move in with me at some point…"

Dora yanked her hand away from him a second time. "I see you all the time," she countered. "It's not like your top-secret biologist Batcave is that far away from Charade — you find your way here at least every other day. And besides, you haven't even taken me to see your cabin yet. It's a bit premature to talk about me moving into it, don't you think?"

"And those animals getting into your stuff!" Lowell added desperately. "That wouldn't happen at the manor. I wouldn't allow it. Aren't you tired of all that?"

Dora climbed out of bed and wrapped a pink velour robe around her body. "I am not the one who has a tantrum every time an animal knocks over a sack of potting soil or a bin of flour," she snapped. "I just clean it up and deal with it, unlike *some* people I know." She yanked her belt around her waist and knotted it tightly. "I'm such an idiot." She crammed her feet into her slippers and wiped her eyes with the back of her hand. "Here I hoped you were going to ask to move in with me at Bohemian Rhapsody. I had no idea you thought it was such a dump." She stormed to the bedroom door and glared at him over her shoulder. "You need to leave, Lowell. This mortal princess is not in the mood for a visit from a bearded god with his head up his ass."

"B-but—" Lowell stammered. "I didn't mean to make you mad."

"Well, you succeeded nonetheless." She gathered his kilt and shirt and tossed them onto his bare stomach. "I'm going to do some cooking in my inadequate and tacky kitchen, so why don't you just hit the road."

Dora padded to her kitchen and poured a glass of cabernet from her wine box. Less than a minute later, Lowell slunk in with his tail between his legs.

"Dora," he began. "I'm sorry. I'm not good at this" — he waved his hand around in the air — "relationship stuff. I just wanted you near me. I wanted to be with you."

"Then you'll just have to keep on wanting," Dora said coldly. "I'm not leaving Bohemian Rhapsody. It may not be perfect, but it's mine, and I love it." She sipped her wine and glared at him. "You should go."

* * * *

Lowell sank back in the bubbling tub and groaned. "Women." He scrubbed hot water on his face with his hands and poured a double handful over his head. "I offered her a perfectly good solution and she acted like I gave her a box of gnome's toenail clippings."

"I resent that!" Mephita snapped. She lifted one gnarled foot from the steaming bath and turned it side to side admiringly. "We dersen't clip our toesies as if they were hedgies or somewhat. We nibbles 'em, all proper-like." She narrowed her eyes and held up her little toe, then drew it towards her open jaws —

"Not in these healing waters you don't!" Lowell said loudly. "It's one thing to share them with gnomes, but quite another to share them with your toenail scraps floating in the water."

Mephita rolled her eyes. "Sheeshies, we dersen't spit them out, a course. We swallows them right up!"

"Ugh, Mephita, that's quite enough." Carmen winced. She ducked her head under the surface of the tub and sat back up, hot water streaming off her short blonde locks. "You were saying, Lowell, that by offering Prescott Manor up to Dora, you were presenting her with a solution?"

"Aye," Lowell grumbled.

"A solution to what, if I might ask?"

Lowell's mouth opened, then snapped shut as he considered.

"Dora doesn't have a problem," Carmen went on. "She lives in the home she loves and she has a boyfriend she enjoys." Brock chuckled and Carmen jabbed him in the ribs with her elbow. "Maybe *you* have a problem, Lowell, but why would Dora know anything about that?"

"Well, I can't tell her about our secrets unless she's willing to move to the woods," Lowell protested weakly, "and I can't very well move in with her since she lives away from the Healing Waters and Living Earth." Water dripped from his beard onto the surface of the bubbling natural hot tub. "My hands are tied."

"She lives not so far, truly. Worth it to go see her, keep her happy, hmm?" a hitherto silent male voice from the far end of the tub offered.

"Ah, just Bufo," Mephita snorted. "That one knows nary and nothing about lovey romantical stuff, just dirt and worms and weeds."

"I'm a cooker, I am!" he retorted indignantly. "Learning to, anyhow."

"You're a mess-maker, from tell I hear." A third gnome slipped off her tunic and stepped into the water. "Best stay to diggering and flower stuffs, you." A drip fell from one of her wide nostrils into the bubbling pool. She sniffled and wiped her nose with the back of one hand.

"Uh, hi there, Limax," Carmen said with a queasy smile. "Brock, I think I'm going to head back to my cottage. Care to join me?" She climbed from the water and headed for the stone chamber designated as the females' changing room.

A bubble surfaced behind Mephita's back and all three gnomes laughed uproariously. "Right behind you!" Brock shouted as he bounded from the tub.

Lowell glared at the three sniggering beings as he rose with as much dignity as he could muster.

"Gnomes," he grumbled under his breath.

He stood by the edge of the pool as water streamed from his naked form. "And you, Bufo," he directed at the male occupant of the tub. "No more slacking off with the Prescott gardens! Do your job, you hear?"

Bufo's eyes fell to the rippling water before him and he nodded quickly.

Scowling, the oldest Rossi son wrapped his kilt around his hips and stalked from the cavern.

* * * *

Lowell grabbed his wrapped parcel and whistled for Dax. Options, each both tempting and utterly unacceptable, teased him as he trudged through the trees. He could tell Dora everything about Prescott Woods so she'd willingly come with him. He could throw her over his shoulder like a caveman and toss her into the Healing Waters and be done with it. Or he could carry on visiting her at Bohemian Rhapsody and endure the antics of the malicious imp that was plaguing the place. Lastly, he could stop seeing her entirely and pay a visit to the dryads in the woods. They'd be glad to help him lick his wounds.

He chuckled, remembering a particularly pleasant woodsy encounter with a couple of trees. Geneva and Hazel were lithe and playful, and free from those aggravating notions that Dora entertained. What foolishness — playing housemaid and cook to complete strangers in a creaking old house, when she could move into an elf-built and gnome-maintained manor?

A flash of lavender caught his eye. "Flowers," he humphed. "She'd like that." He harvested two dozen of the pale purple globes. Then he continued through the trees to Bohemian Rhapsody with a vague plan of presenting her with an impressive bouquet and a gift, then sweeping her off her feet.

* * * *

Dora opened the door at his knock but stood, blocking his entrance and glaring at him.

"I..." Lowell began. "I wanted to see you."

"Well, congratulations." She indicated her robe-clad form with a wave of her hand and cocked her fist on her hip. "You're seeing me."

He cleared his throat and pulled the blooms out from behind his back. "I brought you some flowers from the woods." Lowell grinned triumphantly. "I picked them just for you."

The corner of Dora's mouth twitched. "Smell them," she said in an unsteady voice.

Lowell, baffled, lowered his face to the lavender spheres and inhaled deeply through his nose. "Erm." He searched for words. "They smell...herbal, I'd say? Fresh?"

"Onions, Lowell. You picked onion flowers for me." Dora shook her head and laughed. "Hang on, I'll get a container for them. They'll look pretty on the porch, but they'd stink up the house, I'm afraid."

Lowell sniffed the palms of his hands as he waited. Yup, it was onion all right. Pretty things, but the odour sure did rub off on the skin. Kind of like a certain tumble with a sassafras dryad a few years ago... He grinned in spite of himself.

Dora returned with a vase full of water. She arranged the onion flowers in them. "They do look nice, Lowell," she admitted. "I might add some more blossoms to fill out the arrangement, but those purple flowers will be the centrepiece of it. Thank you. I'm afraid my answer is still the same, though. I'm in no way interested in moving to Prescott Manor, and I'm quite insulted that you would even ask me to."

"Would you give me a chance to explain?" he asked. "And maybe to wash my hands?"

Dora sighed and opened the door wide for him. "Come on in. I don't have any guests today, so there's no one to notice a little eau de onion in the place."

Lowell followed her to the kitchen sink and placed the wrapped box on the counter, then commenced scrubbing his hands with lavender-infused soap.

"The thing is, Dora," he began, "Prescott Woods is unusual. It's a part of me in a way that you can't understand right now." He squished soap between the webs of his fingers. Dora handed him a nailbrush to complete the job. "I am tied to the woods in a way that isn't bad, but that is, ah, permanent." He rinsed the suds from his hands and dried them.

"Well, that's well and good coming from a biologist," Dora said. "It's nice to hear that you're devoted to your career, but, Lowell, I'm devoted to my career, too. I love running Bohemian Rhapsody. Why in the world would I uproot and move?"

Lowell took her hands in his and inhaled deeply, gathering strength for his words. "Dora, I wanted you to move to Prescott Manor with the hope that, eventually, you would move in with me in the woods."

"Have you heard nothing I've been saying?" Dora shook her head and her eyes shone wetly. "I can't run a B&B from a cabin in the woods. What would you expect me to do there—hug trees?"

Lowell stifled a guffaw—Hazel and Geneva would doubtless enjoy that a great deal—and continued. "I wish I could tell you more, but you'll just have to trust me."

Dora pulled her hands away and shook her head. "I'm sorry, Lowell. I like you a lot, I might even..." She sniffled. "But it's not fair of you to ask me to move out of my home and business without giving me a good reason." She tore a paper towel from the holder and blew her nose. "You know, Carmen told me that you could be bossy and irrational. I guess she was right."

"But Dora—"

"I'm sorry, Lowell, but you ought to leave now." She opened the back door for him and looked at the floor. "And this time, don't come back."

Lowell cleared his throat. "Okay, then, I'll tell you the rest of it, Dora. I wasn't going to, I'm not supposed to, but you've left me no choice." He looked over his shoulder, wondering how Gavin would react to what he was about to do. *I know just how he'll react,* Lowell thought grimly. *With disappointment and anger. The real question is, what can Gavin do about it?* Lowell squared his shoulders. *He'll just have to accept it,* Lowell decided. *And if he can't, well, I'll cross that bridge when I get there.*

"The Rossi family is special," he began.

"Yeah, I've seen that. You're weirdly close to your siblings—you all still live a stone's throw away, for Pete's sake. But what does that have to do—"

"No, not special like that. We are the Fair Folk. It's..." He placed one hand on her upper arm and squeezed meaningfully. "It's a kind of magic, Dora."

Dora studied him, confused, then squinted over his shoulder. "Is that a possum on my front porch?" she gaped. "Are you kidding me?"

Lowell whipped his head around and caught a glimpse of a thin, stooped form through the lace panel of Dora's front door.

"Gnome," he glowered. "I should have known." He ran towards the front door, growling with rage. "Gnome! I'm coming for you!"

"Wait, wait!" Dora shouted.

Lowell threw open the front door and grabbed Bufo by the throat. "It was you, you rotting piece of troll dung, lurking about and making mischief—"

"Lowell, what are you doing?" Dora screamed. Lowell, snarling, turned to her with Bufo's skinny body dangling from his grip. She held her hand to her mouth, horrified. "You're a—you're a monster!" she accused. "Anyone who would throttle an innocent possum is..." She shook her head and pointed an angry finger at him. "Not someone I want near me. You let that poor animal go this minute!"

Lowell gritted his teeth and gave Bufo a furious shake. Dora began to sob. "I'm calling the police." She withdrew her cell phone from her pocket and dialled.

"Fine!" Lowell shouted. He flung the whimpering gnome down on the porch floor. "Get out of here, you snivelling piece of crow shit! And hope you don't see me again!"

Bufo scampered out of sight.

"Yes, I'd like to report an instance of animal cruelty," Dora spoke into the phone. "Yes, ma'am. It was Lowell Rossi." She paused. "Well, I'm not sure of his address, other than somewhere in Prescott Woods."

Lowell shook his head in incredulity, then caught a glimpse of the bunch of onion flowers. Oddly, some fern fronds and pieces of trailing variegated ivy had been added to the vase, and some Japanese iris lay scattered on the table before it. Strange.

"Well, it happened right here on my porch at Bohemian Rhapsody. He just up and started throttling a defenceless possum." Dora sniffed. "You should have seen the poor thing. It was scared stiff, little possum feet dangling in the air and pink face just terrified..."

Lowell threw his hands up in the air and left for home.

Chapter Nine

Paul Treble had listened as Dora had described the possum abuse she'd witnessed, then explained politely that, with no injured possum as evidence, there was little he could do. "I can see how that'd be disturbing, ma'am," he'd affirmed. "Poor varmint, all bug-eyed and hissing and whatnot. Bet his little naked, ratty tail was whipping around all over the place." Officer Treble had shaken his head in disgust. "Sounds like the critter got away from Mr Rossi in one piece, though, and since it's not anybody's pet..." He shrugged.

Dora had sent Paul on his way with a frozen loaf of banana bread for his trouble, then locked up the house. "Damn that Lowell Rossi," she mumbled. "Why does he have to be such a nut-job?" She made her way back to the kitchen.

There, on the counter next to the kitchen sink, sat a box wrapped in shiny dark brown paper and tied with a deep green ribbon. "Huh," she muttered, remembering that Lowell had had it under his arm when he'd arrived, along with that bouquet of purple stink blossoms. A rose crafted of heavy ivory paper adorned the box. On one pale petal the name 'Dora' was written in ornate cursive.

She placed the box to her kitchen table and sat down, indecisive. "Oh well," she mumbled. "I don't have to keep it if I don't want it, after all." She untied the satin ribbon and unwrapped the gift.

Nestled in a piece of silky white fabric was an ornate wooden candle holder with a fan-shaped cap on a slender pole. A tissue-wrapped set of slender yellow candles was tucked into the side of the box. "Oh!" Dora breathed. "How lovely, a pyramid windmill." She shook her head, bemused. "This is about the last thing I'd expect a man like Lowell Rossi to give me. Onion flowers seem much more his speed."

At the base of the candleholder was a fairy-tale castle, complete with parapets and an arched front door, surrounded by intricately carved trees. Dora fetched a lighter from a kitchen drawer and set the four beeswax tapers aglow. Within seconds, the fan above the castle started to spin from the flames' rising heat.

Dora spied a tiny, ribbon-wrapped scroll poking out from between two of the trees. She unrolled it and read its contents.

I don't live in a little cabin ~ L.

Dora sank back into her chair, utterly baffled, and watched the pyramid's fan turn. She sank into a reverie, imagining the fantastical goings-on in such a castle—fairies and feasts and enchantments. She could almost hear the lilting music that the elves would play during one of the castle's grand parties and the tinkling laughter of flower sprites.

Suddenly, she had the overwhelming desire for a long, hot bath.

When the tub was nearly full of steaming water, Dora poured in some lily-of-the-valley bath oil and tested the water with one toe. Scorching. *Perfect.*

She stepped into the bath and rested her head on a rolled bath towel. The strange, beautiful pyramid windmill continued to spin on the stool where she'd placed it, right next to the bath. The filmy cloth it had been packed in was arranged beneath it so that the carved scene appeared to float on a white cloud. Dora took a sip from a brimming glass of merlot. "What's your story, Lowell Rossi?" she murmured. The blade moved silently, magically, over the castle's elegant spires.

When the wine glass was drained and the water had cooled somewhat, Dora stood on rubbery legs. A fatigue so intense that it was almost luxuriant fell on her. Bleary-eyed, she stepped from the tub, intent on towelling off and slipping between her covers for a nap.

Her wet feet slid on the tiled floor of the bathroom, however, and Dora's legs flew out from under her. She felt a blinding pain at the back of her head then, strangely, saw a growing yellow light. The fairy-tale castle began to dance in the flames, set aglow by the burning white cloud beneath it, then all faded to darkness.

* * * *

Lowell sat in a bubbling mud bath between his brothers with a snarl on his face. "Can't find the wretched little bugger," he grimaced. "Been through the elf village, the dryad grove and questioned every shifty little gnome I've come across." He glowered. "Probably hiding out with the trolls."

"Bufo's a squirrely little guy. I wouldn't have pegged him for a delinquent, though," Korbin noted. His long hair lay in silt-covered cords on his shoulders.

"Gonna be a flattened delinquent, once I get ahold of him," Lowell grumbled.

"So Bufo was deliberately tearing stuff up and making messes at Dora's place? Doesn't sound like something a gnome would do, does it?" Brock mused. "Are you sure you've got the whole story?"

"Aye, he threw around the flour and the potting soil and the laundry. Creepy little thing, that one. Destructive, messy, sneaky." Lowell grunted. He let his head fall back on the edge of the tub and closed his eyes. "I'll just have to go back and tell Dora everything."

"She might be too scared of you, brother. After all, you're a certified possum-abuser," Brock chuckled.

Lowell ignored him and tried to let the mud ease away his stress. He scrubbed a double handful of the Healing Earth over his face and let its power soak into his skin. It was too much to ask, really. Love a woman enough to want to be with her forever, but not be allowed to reveal the most important aspect of his life? Of course Dora thought he was nuts. He'd just have to tell her everything, get her to understand the real truth, and she'd certainly be willing to relocate to Prescott Woods. She'd be crazy not to. He rubbed the silky mud on his biceps. Maybe get Carmen in on the conversation since Dora trusted her. Yes, it would work. It had to.

"Psssht!" Korbin whispered. "Looks like we've got a visitor."

Lowell furrowed his brows. "Huh?" He wiped the mud from his eyelids, then squinted at a crouched figure near the entrance to the bathing area. "Bufo," he growled. "You've got one hell of a lot of nerve." He stood, mud running down his naked body in rivulets, and cracked his knuckles. "I've been looking for you, gnome."

Korbin and Brock rose and flanked Lowell. The three men emerged, dripping, from the mud bath and surrounded Bufo in a menacing triangle. "You're gonna bitterly regret the day you decided to tangle with the woman I love, gnome. You should have never set one nasty little gnome foot near Bohemian Rhapsody."

"Will you let me go?" he whispered to Brock.

"No," Brock answered, shaking his head grimly. "We will not let you go."

"Let me go!" Bufo beseeched Korbin.

"We will *not* let you go." Korbin glowered.

"Oh, mumsy of mine..." Bufo snivelled and lifted his moist eyes to the ceiling. Visibly shaking, he bobbed his head. "Here I am then, all meekish and 'umble before you Fair Folk devils, knowing for sure and certain that I've done wrong. You to do as you will to poor Bufo—poor, poor Bufo. But first—" The gnome gulped. His knobby Adam's apple slid up and down his throat. "There's trouble. Badness. Burning." He raised his gnarled hands to the stone roof of the chamber and shrieked. "'Tis most frightening!" He fixed his crazed, bulging eyes on Lowell. "Fire at Bohemian Rhapsody!"

"Fire!" Lowell grabbed his kilt as Korbin scooped up his trousers and Brock picked up his hiking shorts. As he buckled his kilt in place, Lowell caught Brock's eye and saw an impish gleam. He smiled grimly as Brock thumped Bufo on the back of his bulbous head, then all three brothers ran from the chamber.

* * * *

Three fire engines, sirens wailing, veered into the drive of Dora's home as the Rossi brothers arrived. A group of neighbours stood silently in the road, watching, with their arms about each other and worried looks on their faces. Bohemian Rhapsody was completely engulfed in flames.

Brock and Korbin paused in the shadows, but Lowell ran full-tilt towards the house. He leapt through a window, sending shards of glass to the ground in a tinkling spray.

"Was that a wolf?" one woman exclaimed. "Did you see that?"

Lowell ran from room to room, hunched and coughing in the smoke. His feet blistered and his lungs screamed for relief. The Iris Room, the Dogwood Room, the Daffodil Room... He stumbled past them all, heading down the hall to the only place that mattered — The Queen Anne's Lace Suite.

The smouldering bed was empty. Lowell, heart thumping, hurried to the bathroom, and there he saw her, spread out on the tiled floor in a room lifted from a nightmare. The walls, the ceiling, the cabinets — all crackled and flamed. Chunks of the ceiling had fallen upon Dora, who lay motionless, her skin cracked and blackened, on the floor. Lowell raised the window in her bedroom, immune to the scalding heat of the sill. He darted back into her bedroom to grab her pink velour robe from its place at the end of her bed and wrapped it around her as he lifted her from the floor. She made no response when he jumped from the window and bore her away from the blazing, doomed structure.

Lowell stuck to the shadows as he ran, not bothering to turn when he noticed Korbin and Brock alongside him. "Is she living, brother?" Korbin asked.

"Of course she is, damn it." Lowell increased his speed when the dark expanse of Prescott Woods entered his sight.

"Where are you taking her?" Brock questioned.

Lowell's bare, blistered feet thudded on the woodland undergrowth. "You have to ask, Brock?" He stole a glance at the pink bundle in his arms. "You, of all people?"

Lowell's body ached and pains assaulted him with every step, but he refused to slow down. At last, Castle Speranza came into sight. Lowell ran past the front door, around the side of his home and past the pond at its rear.

Paloma bolted from the castle and reached the door set into the squat stone archway before he did. "Get out of the way, woman!" Lowell bellowed. "I won't argue with you about this."

She unfastened the bolt on the door and swung it wide. "Just getting the door for you, Lowell," Paloma said sharply, "seeing as your hands are full."

Lowell swept past her and hurried through the torch-lit corridor. He headed towards the more private mud bath and eased onto the rim of the tub. Carmen, out of breath, dashed into the chamber. The robe fell back from Dora's head and Carmen cried out at the sight of her friend's tortured skin and hairless scalp. "Oh my god, it's true," she gasped. "Oh, Dora!"

Lowell opened the front of Dora's robe, but the velour stuck to her burnt skin and tore it, sending a thin trickle of blood over his arms. "Just leave it,"

Carmen said. "The Living Earth will soak through." She splashed into the mud bath, fully clothed, to help Lowell lower himself and Dora into it. "She's still breathing?" Carmen whispered.

Lowell sat in the warm liquid earth and cradled Dora in his arms. His cheeks trembled and he squeezed his eyes closed. "I don't know, Carmen," he forced out. "She hasn't made a sound since I found her."

Carmen moved closer and poured handfuls of mud over Dora's head.

"We'll just have to wait then. I'm in no hurry." She looked up as Brock, Korbin, and Paloma entered the enclosed space. Brock held a goblet in his hands.

"Healing Waters," he said quietly. "For Dora."

Carmen took the vessel from him and held it to Dora's mouth. She tipped it to pour some between her lips, but it dribbled right out again and ran over her chin. Carmen's hand trembled as she placed the goblet on the floor next to the sunken bath. "We'll try again in a little bit," she whispered.

Lowell scooped another handful of mud and let it trickle over Dora's head. "Yes, we will," he agreed.

Brock and Paloma exchanged worried glances.

Chapter Ten

Cock-a-doodle-doo!

Spare Tyre greeted the dawn with his customary enthusiasm. Paloma grabbed a basket from the kitchen and stumbled from the castle, still half asleep. As she reached the door to the bathing chamber, it swung open to reveal Carmen and Brock. "She's breathing." Carmen smiled over red-rimmed eyes. "She swallowed a bit of water, too."

Brock squeezed her shoulder and kissed her cheek. "We're going to get a little shuteye," he told Paloma. "See if you can get Lowell to do the same. He's been up all night holding Dora in the mudbath and I know he's worn out."

"Good luck getting that pig-headed man to take a break," Carmen muttered. "He'll just keep on until he keels over from exhaustion."

Paloma shrugged. "Sounds about right. I've got some rolls, fruit and juice here, so at least he can eat something, if that doesn't break his martyr code of suffering."

"Good luck, Paloma," Carmen yawned. "Korbin said he'd be back this morning, too, after he checked some things out in the library."

Paloma stepped inside the corridor, then turned. "And Father?"

"He spent yesterday settling a troll dispute at the north end of the woods," Brock replied. "If he went straight to bed when he got back, he may not even know about all this…"

Paloma sighed. "He may not know about all this *yet*," she amended. "But there's no question that he *will*." She closed the heavy wooden door behind her and made her way to the bathing chamber.

There, up to his chin in a bubbling pool of warm mud, sat Lowell. He cradled a shrunken form coated in a heavy layer of silt. Paloma was reminded of the apple heads she would make when babysitting young Korbin and Brock while Lowell was off doing some manly thing or other with Father. With her young charges, she'd peeled apples, carved crude features into them, and left them to dry overnight. The next day—presto! There would be shrivelled, gruesome brown faces, mummified apple heads. A raspy breath clattered through the parched lips of the person in Lowell's arms. Paloma shuddered.

"Signs of life, then," she noted. "That's good." She placed the basket on the floor, undressed and entered the tub next to her brother. "Give her to me. You need to stretch, rinse off, go to the bathroom, eat something—" Lowell started to protest, but Paloma cut him off. "Nuh-uh. You're going to get crankier and crankier, and crazier and crazier, and don't you want to be all charming and frisky when Dora wakes up?" She eased Dora from Lowell's embrace, stunned at how bony and fragile the once-curvy woman felt in her arms. "Go on."

Paloma let Dora's head fall against her chest and she smiled encouragingly at Lowell. "It'll be okay," she promised. "I'll take care of her."

Lowell, defeated, rose and walked on stiff legs to the underwater creek. Paloma heard him splash and groan behind her, then dip into the heated pool of Healing Waters. He had to be as puckered as a raisin, but she knew that his body must be craving the magical waters—like the Living Earth, they were essential to his unnaturally vigorous life. Dora's head was still hairless and her eye sockets and cheekbones showed clearly beneath the thin, damaged skin of her face. Paloma ladled warm mud onto her vulnerable scalp.

Splashes from the water tub behind her told her that Lowell was exiting. A few moments later, he stood, dressed in his filthy kilt and mud-smeared T-shirt. "Have some grapes," Paloma offered. "There's apple cider and rolls, too. Do you good."

Lowell hesitated, then dug into the picnic basket. He chugged a bottle of cider and took a single bite of bread. The chamber was silent as he ate except for the trickle of the creek, the faint bubbling in the tubs and the wheeze of Dora's breaths.

Paloma lifted one of Dora's skeletal hands from the mud and started when the bony fingers curled around hers in a shaking grip. "See?" Paloma said excitedly. "She's going to be okay. The mud is healing her."

"No, it's not." A deep male voice rumbled in the corridor. Lowell gulped as Gavin strode into the room. He looked stern and agitated.

"Father," Lowell began. "Please don't be angry. I didn't have any choice. I wanted her to come to the woods anyway, and I think that perhaps she would have of her own accord, but she was burned horribly in a fire." His voice shook. "She would have died if I hadn't brought her here."

Gavin placed one heavy palm on Lowell's shoulder. "I'm not angry, son. You thought you were doing the right thing. What I fear, however..." He gazed down at the gasping creature huddled against Paloma's chest in the pool of mud. "You may have saved her from a death by fire by bringing her to an immortality of pain and suffering. She was not immortal when she received her injuries, so the mud will not restore her to health. It will only keep her from dying."

Lowell swayed on his feet. "But—" he choked out. "She can't just..." A ragged breath cawed from Dora's throat. "She can't just be like this forever." Tears began to run down his face into his beard. "What kind of a life would that be?"

Shaking his head, Gavin pressed the heels of his hands into his eyes, and replied in a quiet voice. "Not a life she would have chosen, son."

Lowell's head dropped into his hands and he sobbed openly, broad shoulders shaking. "What can I do?" he gasped. "Oh god, what have I done? I promised her I'd never let anything hurt her, Father."

Gavin's jaw clenched and he cleared his throat. "Oh, son," he murmured. "I'm sorry." He wrapped his arms around Lowell and held him as he cried.

Paloma's throat felt as dry as old bones. She swallowed with effort and looked down at the horribly burnt woman she held. Cradled in the foetal position, Dora was as weak as a kitten. *What's she thinking?* Paloma wondered. *Does she understand what's going on? Is she frightened?* She felt hot tears sting her eyes. *Is she hurting?*

"Don't worry, Dora," she whispered. "I'm going to take care of you. It's going to be okay. I'm not sure how yet." Paloma raised the goblet of healing water to Dora's lips and let a few drops trickle into her mouth. "But it will. I promise."

* * * *

Hours later, Lowell, incoherent with sorrow, finally succumbed to Paloma's repeated request that he sleep. He had refused to rest in the castle, but had agreed to lie down on a pallet near the mud bath. Paloma watched the huge man, racked by grief and remorse, stretch out. The improvised bed could hardly have been comfortable—just a thin pad on top of the hard stone floor, with a pillow and a blanket to soften it— but his body was depleted by strain. His red-rimmed eyes, fixed on Dora in Paloma's arms, struggled to stay open, but fatigue won out. Within minutes, he was snoring lightly.

Carmen, bearing a couple of folded blankets, returned to take a shift holding Dora. She was surprised that the Living Earth hadn't restored her friend yet, and Paloma didn't have the heart to tell her that it wouldn't. "It must just take longer to heal someone who is new to being one of the Fair Folk," Carmen said. "Her injuries were really bad, after all."

"Mm-hm," Paloma hummed in reply. "Must be." She rinsed herself in the creek and took a brief dip into the Healing Waters before drying and dressing herself. Uncorking a bottle of cider from her basket, she leant back against the cavern wall and drank.

"You can go, you know," Carmen told her. "I'm sure you need some rest yourself." She inclined her head towards Lowell and grinned slightly. "It does a body good."

"Oh, thanks, but I think I'll stay." Paloma shrugged. "I know Dora's your friend and all, but I feel rather protective of her. I…" Once more, Paloma felt a queer, painful dryness in her throat and a sharp stinging in her eyes. "I want to see her get better." A noisy breath rattled from between Dora's lips.

"You're funny, you know that?" Carmen shook her head. "All prickles and thorns, but you've got a soft heart under there, don't you?"

Paloma sighed. "Oh, I'm still a bitch, don't you worry. It's just that Dora's a nice person." She bit her lip. "She doesn't deserve this."

"Well, she'll get better soon," Carmen said. "And then she'll be one of the Fair Folk. Might take some adjusting, but I'm guessing it will all work out beautifully."

Paloma squeezed her eyes shut to hide the tears that sprang up in them. Thankfully, Carmen's attention was on Dora and she didn't see her expression.

Chapter Eleven

Running footsteps clattered into the bathing chamber. Korbin, platinum hair dishevelled, raced in with a heavy book in his hands. "She needs water," he panted. "Healing Water. The Living Earth has brought her back, but now she needs to heal."

Carmen drew her eyebrows together. "We've been giving her sips of water," she said. "I thought the mud was more important right now."

"No, no." Korbin held aloft the battered tome. "This happened once before to a gnome. Well, to a gnome's girlfriend. He fell in love with a human woman..." Korbin scanned the pages with his fingertip and read aloud from the book. "'A human female of short stature, notable body fragrance, ample calluses and well-defined earlobes.'"

"A gnome pin-up girl," Brock muttered.

"Indeed. Seems that he lured her into Prescott Woods and was just about to douse her with Healing Water and Living Earth when she stepped into a tangle of roots and broke both of her legs." Korbin made a tsk-tsk sound.

"Damn dryads. Probably got jealous." Lowell grunted as he sat up on his pallet, listening. He yawned and fluffed his beard.

"We'll never know—perhaps it was a simple accident. At any rate, the gnome dumped her straight into this mud bath and, while it did awaken her senses and give her the rush of immortality, her legs were still twisted and unusable. Poured water over her head, too, to no effect."

"Did her broken legs still hurt her?" Paloma asked quietly.

"Um"—Korbin squinted at the book in his hands—"doesn't say. At any rate, the gnome had a flash of insight."

"You're kidding me," Lowell muttered. "Gnomes don't have insights." He took an apple from Paloma's picnic basket and crunched into it.

"This one did. He saw that the Healing Water had touched her too late to fix her legs—they were already broken when she'd been changed—so he needed to get some water that had passed by prior to her conversion."

"Huh? It's all the same water." Carmen shook her head, confused. "I don't understand."

Korbin licked his lips. "There's a lot we don't know about Prescott Woods, Carmen. We've lived here for over two centuries, but the history books that the elves kept are practically indecipherable, and they're the only ones who kept any records at all. It could be that there's something intrinsic to this layer of Earth's crust, something embedded in the topmost rock here, so that when the water and mud trickle through..." His eyes shone with interest. "You know, *my* theory is that—"

"Later!" Lowell bellowed. "Theories later, damn it. How can we help Dora?" He tossed the apple core back into the basket and sat at the edge of the mud bath next to his sister. Dora's wheezing breaths continued, but she remained still in Paloma's lap.

"The gnome grabbed his lady friend and jumped into the stream. He carried her downstream with him, where the stream winds through the rocks far underground, until he reached the water that had passed through the cavern at precisely the moment she'd been converted to a magical being," Korbin said, his speech quickening. "The water that passed through magical layers of Prescott Wood's floor at the exact time his girlfriend was injured was the only thing that could heal her, and it *did*."

Carmen looked up at Brock with a pained expression. "Dora's not healing right now?" He took her hand and kissed her knuckles.

"Not healing, just living," Lowell answered grimly. "How did the gnome know when he'd gotten to the right water, Korbin?"

Korbin chuckled. "She started kicking the hell of out him. I'm guessing that the relationship was a little one-sided, at that point anyway."

"Creepy little stalker gnome." Paloma shuddered.

"Well then." Lowell stood. "We don't have any time to waste. I'll take Dora into the underground stream, as far as I need to. When she gets better..." He glanced at her shrivelled, mud-coated form. "I'll know it."

"Not so fast," Korbin said. "You're too big, Lowell. Dora's too big, too. This book said that the gnome and his lady friend had to squeeze through some places. 'Wiggling like fish and writhing like snakes through the rocks. Only by exhaling all his breath and pushing on fearlessly through the bleak, lightless, watery path could the gnome proceed'. You'll never fit."

"We need a little person, tiny enough to negotiate those twists and turns for miles and miles." Carmen looked down at Dora with a hopeless expression. "Someone brave and committed to the task. Someone who won't turn around, no matter what."

"We need a gnome," Paloma stated.

Someone coughed lightly in the archway of the corridor, then emerged into the flickering torchlight. "You ones need *me*." He thumped his chest with one gnarled finger and nodded. "Bufo's your gnome."

"You." Lowell's hands balled into fists and he took a step towards him.

Bufo stood, unwavering, and nodded. "Me. This one here is most special." He indicated Dora with a tilt of his misshapen head. "Worth a splooshy plunge and twisty swim into the deep unknown."

"But how will he get the right water to Dora?" Carmen wondered. "He can't bottle it up to bring back when he doesn't know where it'll be."

"With this he will!" a female voice cackled. Limax entered behind Bufo and held up a coiled tube. "Knew all this, we did, and how to fix it, so had those elves concoct a squirter on the hurry-up!" She caught Bufo's eyes with hers and giggled. "Elves and trolls and us have been busy, uh-huh and sure enough."

Korbin took the tube from her and examined it. He tugged the free end and stretched it to arm's length. "Remarkable," he whispered. "It doesn't flatten or thin or anything, just grows in length."

"Yuh-uh." Limax agreed with a sniffle. "Clevery elves, eh? Told them to make it so it'll scrapey-bump over rocks and no tearing, twisty-slide through tight spots and no trouble, gotsa keep the water flowing, no stops! Been busy, yah, creatin' and suchlike."

"Okay, then, Bufo," Korbin told the gnome. "You're going to have to go downstream holding this tube, for who knows how far." He shook his head. "I just hope you don't get blocked or stuck. When you've gone far enough, when we see Dora start to improve, we'll tug on our end. Move at the same rate as the water for another ten minutes or so, then come on back when we tug again."

The gnome took the end of the hose in his fist and strode into the rushing stream. "Best off then!" Bufo took a deep breath and disappeared into the rock tunnel.

"Ah, brave one, he." Limax's eyes welled with tears and she wiped her nose on the back of her hand.

"Let's move Dora into the water tub," Korbin advised, "since it's water she needs now."

Lowell strode into the mud bath, kilt flopping in the silty ripples, and lifted Dora from Paloma's arms, then walked with her to the tub. Paloma rinsed off in the stream and slipped her dress over her head, then followed. "The water's going to wash the coating of mud away," she said quietly. "She's burnt badly, Lowell."

"I know," he answered. A cloud of fine clay spread from Dora's form when Lowell lowered her into the tub. Still wrapped in her robe, her body was mercifully hidden, but her head and hands were uncovered and still caked with mud.

Korbin held the free end of the hose up to her neck and a rush of clear water revealed a strip of cracked, raw skin on her collarbone. "We'll just keep the running water here for now. When her skin starts to heal, we'll see it, and then we can cleanse the rest of her body." He stared soberly at the damaged skin beneath the stream that ran from the hose.

Carmen, Paloma and Brock sat around the rim of the tub and dangled their feet in the water. "This will probably take a while, you know. Bufo will have to swim faster than the water is flowing. He'll have to work his way through who-knows-what..." Lowell closed his eyes.

"Good swimmer, Bufo is," Limax soothed. "Quick and slippery as a froggie in a pond, yes."

"He'd better be," Lowell said grimly. Dora's breath rattled, then calmed. The water from the hose flowed over her tortured skin.

The Fair Folk sat in grim silence, their combined attention focused on Dora's injured body and a slim trickle of water. They waited. Carmen shifted her weight from side to side and Brock gave her hand a squeeze.

From deep within the earth, splashes and shouts echoed up to the bathing cavern. Lowell ground his jaw until his teeth squeaked together.

"Hope he's not hurt," Paloma whispered. "Or stuck."

Brock rolled his shoulders and cracked his knuckles. Lowell glared at him, then cradled Dora to his chest protectively.

Carmen glanced around the room at each tense face. She cleared her throat. "I know we can't see the sky down here, but we can imagine the moon shining down on us, right? It's a blue one tonight, you know. Second full moon this month. But then, the moon's always blue in Kentucky, right?" Lowell's brows lifted with interest. "I always loved this song—I think it helped me find my way to Charade."

Carmen began to sing 'Blue Moon of Kentucky', the rollicking bluegrass waltz made famous by Bill Monroe and, later, by a black-haired king from Memphis with a crooked smile. Paloma's eyes shone. "I remember dancing to this with Calvin," she whispered. "He stepped on my feet!"

Korbin hummed along, letting the hose end sway in time to the music. Brock and Carmen harmonised as Paloma snapped along. Lowell swayed in the bubbling tub, sending ripples across his siblings' calves.

By the time they reached the end of the song, the mood of the room had lightened considerably. All the Fair Folk present—Brock, Carmen, Paloma, Korbin and Lowell—sang the last lines together.

"Look! Look, you guys!" Lowell shouted. "Oh my God, her skin! It's healing!" Beneath the clear flow from the tube, Dora's skin had changed from a charred, angry red-black to a blushing pink.

Korbin gave the hose three brisk yanks. "Stand up with her, Lowell, hold her steady!" Lowell, his face a mask of shock and joy, rose and held Dora in the bubbling pool. Korbin lifted the tube to her head first, letting the water stream over her head and face. The mud rinsed away, and for a gruesome split-second her burned flesh was visible, but within the span of a heartbeat the injured tissue mended and smoothed. Carmen wept and ran her hands over Dora's scalp as her glossy black hair grew back—lustrous, thick and wavy.

Dora's lips plumped and filled out beneath the healing rivulet, and her eyelashes sprouted as her eyelids fluttered open. "Wha...? Whazzit?" she slurred.

"Hush," Paloma murmured, tears welling in her eyes. "Just hush and be still, Dora."

Korbin rinsed her robe-shrouded body, then eased the sodden fabric from her skin. Naked, her exposed pink skin glowed with health. Carmen took the hose from Korbin as Lowell held Dora like a doll in his wide hands beneath the gentle flow. Moving slowly, Carmen directed the stream under Dora's arms, beneath her breasts, under her feet, between her toes and fingers, and between her legs. "Good," Lowell urged. "Be thorough, Carmen. I don't want her to have any scars or pain from this."

Carmen gave Dora's face, scalp and neck a last dose of Healing Water. She sprayed water in Dora's ears and nostrils, then parted her lips to rinse her mouth. "Swallow," Carmen said. "You need some of this, my friend."

Dora covered Carmen's hand with her own, holding the tube to her lips, and drank deeply. She smiled drunkenly. "Yum," she chuckled. Her eyes rolled back and her head lolled on her shoulders. Korbin yanked on the hose a second time.

Paloma and Carmen, weeping and smiling, wrapped a woozy Dora in a fluffy blanket. A splash erupted from the streambed and Bufo's bug-eyed face popped into view. He looked at Dora, limp and lovely, in Lowell's arms and hooted in triumph.

"Good job, Bufo," Carmen said. She smiled at the rejoicing gnome. "Well done."

Lowell's cheeks gleamed with tears. "She's okay! I'll take her to the castle, then, and let her rest."

"But she'll restie better at her place, will she not?" Limax asked. "In her ownsie bed and under that familiar roof of hers own?"

"Bohemian Rhapsody burned down, Limax," said Carmen. "That's the last place Dora needs to be."

The patter of feet echoed down the entry corridor as another visitor arrived. An elf, taller than the gnomes and more elegantly proportioned, bowed curtly. "The first wing, which includes her suite, is complete." he stated in a high-pitched voice. "Follow me."

Bufo cackled with delight.

"What've you done now, gnome?" Lowell glowered.

"Oh, go on, you, and take a look-see." Bufo crawled from the stream and shook his head like a dog. "You'll be smilin', betcha five chickens you will."

Lowell followed the gnome down the flame-lit corridor.

Korbin turned to Bufo. "Do you have a few moments to spare?" he asked. "I'd love to record your subterranean experiences while they're fresh."

Bufo accepted another blanket from Carmen and followed Korbin from the cavern. "Oh, eeesh, wormsies and lightsies and teeniney fairy folk and awfullish things with teeth." he began. "And wheels and wires, like the guts of a clock, moving and clicking, right beneath rock and pebble, as though 'twere living bones rolling about under skin."

Paloma, Brock and Carmen dried their feet as Limax, who was eager to extol Bufo's virtues, chattered away. "At home in wet and dry he is!" she crowed. "And a jumper like none you've seen, and can snarf up the flies like a snappin' fish, that one can…"

As she left the chamber, Carmen glanced at the man in a shadowy corner of the bathing chamber. She nodded at him, but spared him the attention he clearly wanted to avoid. She knew that Gavin would leave last and alone, ever the stern patriarch of the clan, and wondered if his children would ever know the tangle of emotions that lay beneath their father's calm exterior.

Chapter Twelve

Dora sat up and stretched. Her bed linens had never felt so luxuriantly silky, nor the mattress so perfectly firm yet supple. The sunlight streamed in through her white lace curtains and songbirds chirruped outside. She felt rested, energetic and healthy. "Feels like I've had a massage and a twelve-hour nap." She ran her fingers through her hair. "Awesome."

She looked down at a hulking form curled beneath her green-sprigged sheets. "Lowell?" she wondered aloud. "You slept here?"

Lowell snorted and rubbed his face. He grinned sleepily. "Hope you don't mind. You were a little, ah, well... Let's just say you were as inviting as all get-out, and I couldn't bear to leave you alone."

Dora lay on her side and propped herself on one elbow. "Is that so, Lowell Rossi?" She ran her hands down his side and tugged the sheet down to his hip bone. "I'll confess that last night is a bit of a blur. Last thing I remember is you being aggressive with a possum and leaving when I called the cops, and then me settling in to a bath with some wine." She smiled to see a familiar shape grow beneath the crisp sheets.

"Well, perhaps you had more wine that you realised—" Lowell began. He froze when Dora's hand found his erection and gripped it.

She smiled and stroked him through the sateen cotton. "Were you watching me in the tub through my bathroom window, hoping to make amends?" she asked. Lowell's shaft hardened in her grip. "I ought to be mad at you for what you did to that poor possum, but all I can think about is how good I feel..." She licked her lips and tossed her sleep-tousled hair over her shoulder. "And how good *you* feel."

"Ah, Dora, there's something we should talk about," Lowell said. "Some things you need to know." He groaned as Dora lifted her legs and straddled him. She pulled the sheet away and pressed his cock against the dark curls of her pubic hair.

"I don't want to talk." She placed one palm on his chest and raised herself up slightly on her knees. "I want to feel this thing..." She rubbed the tip of his shaft down her belly until it found her opening. "I want to have it inside of me, shoved to the hilt, and I want you to pound it in me until I scream."

Lowell grabbed her rear with both hands and nodded. "I can do that."

Dora settled herself onto his erection and let her eyes fall closed. "Here," she whispered. "Right here, Lowell, is where you belong." She eased down onto him slowly, letting his girth stretch and fill her, and hummed contentedly. "Don't you agree?" She smiled.

"Absolutely." He growled and took one breast in each hand. "Come on then, woman. Don't just sit there." He pinched her nipples between thumb and index finger and tilted his hips up to her.

She leaned over him and let her breasts swing towards his face, then began to pump her hips. "You're so thick," she murmured, "so heavy. I love it."

Lowell caught one peak in his mouth as she ground on top of him. Her free breast brushed over his face, the taut nipple stroking his closed eyes, his nose, his cheeks.

"Yeah," she breathed. She spread her thighs wider, craving more of his fat shaft. The bed creaked under her as she bucked into his body. "Suck it."

Lowell pulled her breast harder into his mouth. She pumped faster, torn between the sweet, stretching tug of his mouth on her tit and the thick tightness of his cock in her cunt.

She cried out as she came, a guttural animal scream, and slammed down on his shaft. "There!" she gasped. "Right there, Lowell!" Her body shuddered in his grip.

He grabbed her around the waist and flipped her trembling body over. "Don't stop," he murmured. "Keep coming, Dora." He shoved his length into her, grunting with each stroke. The headboard of the bed thumped against the wall. Energy thrummed through her, then the intensity of her orgasm receded slightly and she opened her eyes. Lowell was on top of her, jaw clenched and teeth bared. "Get ready," he forced out. She wrapped her ankles around his lower back and tilted her hips up to him. The slap-slap of flesh on flesh was loud, but the rush in Dora's ears drowned it out.

Another climax drew tantalisingly closer. "Harder," she urged. "Faster."

Lowell squeezed his eyes closed and roared, pummelling into her. Dora came again and raked her nails across his back. The room tilted and every nerve in her body sang out. He tensed, groaning, then slumped onto her body, breathing hard.

She waited a moment before rolling his heavy body off her. "That was amazing, Lowell, but whew! I am completely ravenous. What would you say to some pumpkin bread and tea, Lowell? Maybe some pistachios and cheese, too. I feel like I could eat a horse." She picked up her robe where it was draped across the bench at the foot of the bed and frowned, fingering the material thoughtfully. "Huh. They must have improved the brand of laundry softener I use," she murmured. "My robe feels like it's brand new. Weird." She knotted it around her waist and stood. "What the hell? My rug feels especially thick and plush, too, and it looks like my chandelier was just polished, but I know I haven't done that in months." She laughed lightly. "Oh well, if I'm losing my mind, I suppose this is a nice way to go."

"Dora, there's something we should talk about." Lowell chewed his lip and stared at the ceiling. "Something you ought to know."

"Food first!" Dora insisted. "I'm going to fold in half and disappear if I don't get something to eat." She bounded into the hallway, then paused. "Holy hell, the ceilings look higher than they used to," she muttered. "And the wood floors are all glossy, as if they've been refinished..."

Lowell lurched nude from her bedroom and grabbed her in the hall just outside the kitchen. "Wait!" he ordered. "Just wait, okay? This is important."

Baffled, Dora studied his face. "Well, okay then. Spit it out! Did you have a cleaning crew in here while I was sleeping or what?" She leant back against the wall and waited.

Lowell took a deep breath and scratched the back of his neck. His mouth dropped open, then snapped shut again. Dora laughed. "No rush, I guess. You're easy on the eyes, after all." She ran her hands down his stubbled neck, over his wide chest and ridged abdomen. "Just don't forget you're dealing with a woman who's got a powerful appetite." She wriggled her shoulders against the wall to scratch them. "Damnation, I'm itchy! Feels like something's been chewing on me. Oooh, what is that?" She yanked her robe down to her elbows and turned her bare back to Lowell. "Poison ivy?"

Lowell raised one hand to her skin and touched it lightly. "Um, Dora," he began. "This is going to be hard for you to believe. You need to take a look, then let me help you understand what you're seeing."

"If you say so." Dora rolled her eyes and moved in front of the full-length mirror in the hallway. Turning, her eyes widened when her back came into view. Two brilliant pink scars, both in the shape of spread hands, covered her ribs beneath each armpit. She squinted at the reflection. "My skin looks twisted and bumpy, almost like it's been burnt. What in the world?"

Holding her gaze with a sad expression, Lowell stood in front of her and placed his two hands over the scars — they fit the outlines perfectly. Then he lifted her off the floor. "This is how I held you when we restored your skin with Healing Water. I guess my hands kept it from soaking in, in these two spots." He lowered her and kissed her lips before settling her back on her feet. "Your skin was like that — well, a lot worse, actually — all over, but the magic of Prescott Woods saved you."

Dora looked back over her shoulder at her scarred back, then brought her hands to her cheeks and took a deep breath. She rested her palms on his chest and looked up at him. "Tell me, Lowell," she said quietly. "Tell me everything."

"Let's go to your greenhouse and sit by the fountain," he said, humour crinkling at the corners of his eyes. "And we should go ahead and get something to eat on the way, I guess. Let me grab my kilt..."

Dora pulled her robe back into place and stared after him. "Greenhouse?" she muttered. "I don't have a greenhouse."

* * * *

Two hours later, Dora and Lowell sat beside each other on an intricate wicker settee. Their feet, along with a coffee pot, cups, plates and a tray of goodies, rested on the table before them. Behind them, a three-tiered marble fountain burbled and a lush array of potted plants adorned the shelves. Dora stared out the spotless glass wall and over the lawn into Prescott Woods. "So, I have new a new neighbour now," she said. "Bobby Carter, huh?"

"Yup." Lowell sipped his coffee. "But all that he can see right now is a house under construction. We've placed a glamour on this place so that people don't get worried about how it came up so fast."

"Uh-huh. Wouldn't want everybody demanding elven, gnome and troll labour, would you?" Dora nodded. "And Calvin Prescott doesn't mind me being here?"

"Well, it's none of Calvin Prescott's business, to be honest. The woods belong to my family, and Calvin is just the current human caretaker." Lowell took Dora's hand in his and brushed his lips against her knuckles. "But no, Calvin is quite fond of you and is delighted with this turn of events. To be honest, I think he hopes that having you here will help keep intruders away. Even with the magic we use to keep mortals from setting foot in the woods, some idiots still wander in from time to time. Apparently some photographer sneaked in and had a run-in with a leprechaun and his pot of gold not long ago."

"And it was Calvin's gardener, Bufo, who helped with this place's creation? When will I get to meet him?"

Lowell scowled, then shook his head. "Dumbass gnome," he grunted. "Guess he had a thing for you and was sneaking over, wanting to help out."

"With planting, cleaning, weeding, decorating. I welcome that kind of help, Lowell." Dora shot Lowell a sharp look. "But it seems that somebody went barrelling after him and scared him."

"Creepy little dude, lurking around. Should've made his presence known, is all I can say. Not my fault if he's scared of me."

"Mm-hm." Dora picked up a piece of shortbread and nibbled.

"Well, he turned out to be useful in the end, I'll admit. Not only was he slippery and small enough to get the Healing Waters you needed from deep underground, he was crucial to the reconstruction of your home. Who knew that gnomes had such good memories? He was able to describe your decorations and knick-knacks perfectly to the elves so that they could make copies. Huh. Funny little guys are smarter than they look. He even dug up the roots of your blaze roses and transplanted them here, along with the peonies and irises." Lowell pressed his lips on her knuckles. "The rest of the guest rooms will be done soon, and of course you can provide all the input you like. They're taking the day off, at my request, to make sure you get all the rest you need." He tucked a lock of her hair behind her ear. "You're taking all this rather well, you know," he observed. "Your house burnt down and you're forever tied to Prescott Woods and my family. You can't ever live anywhere else — doesn't that bother you?"

Dora considered before she spoke. "Charade is where I belong, Lowell. You may not know this, but it's my first and only real home. My parents sent me to various boarding schools and summer camps — whichever was cheapest — as I was growing up. They travelled around and didn't have much money, so I shouldn't blame them, but I ended up feeling like I had no roots. Then they died and I was left with nothing at all, not even a family house." She chewed and swallowed a bite of cookie. "I stumbled upon Charade and knew I'd found what I was looking for. I made my own home here, filled it with heirlooms I bought for myself and surrounded myself with a family of friends. I'd never choose to leave this place."

She ran her fingertips down his cheek and brushed his lips with a feather-soft touch. "Bufo sounds a little kooky and sneaky, sure, but the fact that he — that your whole family of magical folk in the woods — would so painstakingly rebuild my house for me is..." She shook her head and swallowed past the lump in her throat. "It's the family I've always wanted, Lowell. Risking it all to save me, then going out of their way just to put me at ease." Dora let her head fall back on the couch cushion and took in one shaking breath. "It's like I was in love with this place already, throwing my arms out to it and giving it my all, and then suddenly it swept me right off my feet and hugged me right back. I'm honoured to be linked to

Prescott Woods and the beings there, Lowell. And you, Mr Rossi, you made this all happen. Perhaps it's not what I'd planned, but your magic saved my life — and lengthened it immeasurably. I'm not going to complain about my house burning down when I get to live a new, bigger, better version, plus I get free gardening and cleaning!" She giggled. "I mean, it's like a dream come true!"

"Well, there's one little catch. We could probably work around it if we wanted to, I guess, but..." His face reddened over his beard. "The idea was that we were only to permit people to be converted to Fair Folk if they, uh..."

"Agreed to live together? Be mates? Is that what you're saying?"

"Ah, well, it was Father's idea, but it was one that we all agreed to live by. All of us Rossis, that is." He swallowed, cheeks flaming red. "I had decided that I, ah, wanted you...that is, if you wanted me, but I needed you to agree to move to the woods with me first before I told you our secrets."

"But now I live here, with the woods in my backyard, and you said the elves have built a new bathing chamber for me just inside the trees." Dora pursed her lips. "I don't need to move with you to your family's home."

"Well, no," Lowell admitted. "You don't. You can run your business here, have guests as you used to, as soon as enough time has elapsed for this house to have conceivably been built by human hands. You can go to the Healing Waters and Living Earth by yourself. You don't have to go with me. The only requirement, really, is that you keep the magic of Prescott Woods a secret." He stared at his knees.

The splash of the fountain filled the long moments that followed.

"But what if I didn't want to be alone?" Dora wondered aloud. "What if I wanted company? Someone who could help me run this place, someone to show me around the woods and introduce me to the magic beings there…"

Lowell's face lit up. "Someone to warm your bed, perhaps, my queen?"

Dora tilted her head to one side, considering. "I'd want more than that," she told him. "I'd want someone to take care of me and be my partner. Someone to fix meals for and spend time with. Someone who would—" She looked at him carefully. "Love me."

"I do, Dora, I do!" he burst out. At once, Lowell was off the couch, shoving the table out of the way, and on his knees before her. "Dora, I'm a bumbling fool when it comes to sentimental words, but I can say this." He took her hands in his and squeezed. "I love you. I will always love you. You are everything I've ever wanted in a wife." Dora stroked his black beard and smiled as he spoke. "I love the way you cook and keep house. I love your sweet collections of cups and aprons and frilly stuff." Dora giggled, blushing wildly. "And God knows I love your body." He ran his hands up her ribs and hefted one breast in each hand. "Mm, woman, when you dance and move this body of yours…" he growled.

"Wait a sec—" Dora held his hands still. "Was that a marriage proposal? Did you just ask me to marry you, Lowell Rossi?"

Lowell nodded. "I did, Dora Fontaine. Will you marry me and share an enchanted life with me here? Will you let me love you and protect you forever?"

Dora nodded, eyes glowing. "I will. I'll welcome you into my home—*our* home—today and every day, and be your wife, Lowell." She lowered her face and found his mouth with hers. His beard tickled her as his lips parted and his tongue flicked against hers. A rush of warmth ran from the top of Dora's head down to her toes. She parted her knees to him and sighed.

He untied her robe and slid it down her arms. "I was so afraid you'd never be healed," he whispered, tracing his fingers over the curves of her stomach. "Terrified that your life had not ended, but been ruined for all time, and now to have you here in my arms, beautiful and whole and promised to me." He thumbed her nipples and licked his lips. "I've never been happier in my life."

Dora cried out when he pulled one nipple into his mouth, sucking hard. She held his head to her chest and gasped when he placed one hand between her legs. "No one's here?" she asked.

"Mm," Lowell answered. He nipped her peak with his teeth before releasing it. "No one at all. Humans would see a house under construction, and, should they be stupid enough to set foot here, they'd find a nest of snakes to greet them." He chuckled. "And my family knows to give us some space. I wanted to explain the situation to them." He turned to the other breast, rolled it between finger and thumb then pulled it between his lips.

Dora raked her nails through his hair. "Does everybody in town think I burnt up?" she asked suddenly. "Oh, that's horrible. Poor Colby and Deb, Monica and Bernice." Lowell gave her nipple one last tug with his mouth, then released it and sat beside her.

"Nobody found your body in the ashes, of course, so folks in Charade have been talking up a storm, according to Carmen. However, when it was clear last night that you were going to recover from your injuries, Carmen told your friends and the police that she'd heard from you. Said you were off visiting friends in North Carolina and were all torn up about your place." He placed one arm around her shoulders and pulled her close to him. "When you're ready, you can go back into town and see what's left of Bohemian Rhapsody." He kissed the top of her head. "I'll go with you."

She snuggled into his shoulder and peered into the shadowy woods. "You know what I want to do first?" she said. "I want to see your home and thank your family for their help. And I want to meet these gnomes I've heard so much about."

"Damn gnomes…" Lowell muttered darkly.

"The rate you were going, we'd have ended up together around my eightieth birthday." Dora shrugged. "Bufo sort of hurried things along." He grunted. "All's well that ends well, Lowell." She rubbed her hand over his chest and considered. "So, I can't have guests here for the time being and I can't leave the woods for very long. I'm not up for looking at the ruins of my home just yet, either. Looks like we've got some time on our hands, huh? Whatever should we do, Lowell?"

"Oh, I've got an idea or two," Lowell answered. "A little pre-wedding trip, if you're up for some adventure. It'll introduce you to some of the inhabitants of the woods that you haven't met yet, too. I'm sure they'll be thrilled with your company."

"I'm intrigued," smiled Dora. "Anything I should pack?"

"Ah, you won't need much," he said. "We can send some gnomes for food and water, so just bring what you'll need for a few days." His eyes narrowed and he shot her a concerned look. "I know you're not shy, but you're not afraid of heights, are you?"

Epilogue

Dora stretched beneath the canopy of leaves. The morning sun filtered through the branches and, far below her on the ground, woodland creatures and magic folk shifted and scurried. The nocturnal beings — the sprites and will-o-the-wisps, bats and raccoons — were headed to bed, while the daytime creatures stirred from their burrows to welcome the sun. She imagined the day shift and night shift workers in an otherworldly factory exchanging pleasantries and yawning as they punched their time cards.

"Be right back," she whispered to Lowell, who dozed next to her.

"Down please, Geneva!" she called out. The juniper tree whispered and shuffled, and its limbs bent and swayed to form a living stairway to the ground. *As long as I live,* thought Dora, *even if it's forever, this place will never stop being magical.*

The branches shifted beneath her feet, and Dora climbed down the organic escalator with ease. It had been just a few days since she'd awakened in her transformed state, but she felt completely trusting of the dryad who helped her down to the forest floor. "Geneva's flighty at times," Lowell had confided, "but she's a sweet spirit. Hazel's nice, too, though she can be a bit of a nut. Some of these dryads are tricksters — not that that's a bad thing, of course — but let's stay in Geneva's branches for our first visit to the grove."

Dora heeded the call of nature and freshened up in an overland stream next to the grove. The water in Prescott Woods, even the surface variety, was especially pure and cleansing. She rinsed her teeth and body, combed her hair with her fingers and caught her reflection in a still part of the brook. Dora brought her fingers to her cheek and stared at her mirror image. Her skin was smooth and taut, her body firm and curvy, and her hair looked as though J. Lo's stylist had spent hours on it. The magical properties of Prescott Woods had gifted her with an idealised outward appearance and, even better, she *felt* like a million bucks. *I think I could run for miles, climb a mountain, swim a lake...* She looked up to find Lowell gazing down at her from their treetop hammock. *And then make love with Lowell for hours.*

The phone lines at the new Bohemian Rhapsody were already in place, so Dora had made a few reassuring calls to her friends and family before setting off into the woods with Lowell. He had taken her to Castle Speranza first to see his family and to meet Limax, Mephita and the infamous Bufo. Lowell's father had been surprisingly emotional given Lowell's description of the Fair Folk's stern patriarch. Gavin had embraced her, nearly squeezing the breath out of her, and Dora was sure she'd seen him wipe tears from his eyes as he'd walked away. Paloma, whom Dora knew from belly dancing classes and performances, seemed different than before — kinder, perhaps. Along with Korbin and Brock, she'd welcomed Dora warmly into the family. Carmen was the most ebullient of the bunch. She'd shrieked with joy when Dora and Lowell announced their plans to marry. "We're going to have so much fun, you wait and see!" she'd laughed.

Aside from some rather off-putting sinus issues, Limax was charming enough, and Mephita entertained her with a recounting of her part in saving the woods from destruction. It was Bufo, though, who revealed his deep affection for her. The guilt-ridden gnome had flopped at her feet and begged forgiveness for his transgressions. "You did say as you thought my gardening was clever, and then I wanted to see what your own plantsies were doing, and I saw somewhat and other I could do to improve your place and..." he wailed. "I never did mean to crack a breaksie or dirty not a thing for you, only to pretty up and work for you, and then that horrible fire! Oh, so very, very frightening!"

With Calvin's blessing, Bufo agreed to be head gardener for Dora's new home. Lowell had grudgingly agreed to the arrangement on one condition — Bufo was not to enter Dora's house unless lives were in danger. Dora, as grateful as she was for Bufo's brave part in saving her, was secretly relieved. He was a nice gnome, certainly, but he seemed a bit star-struck by her. Bufo's sister, Caudata, would be her housekeeper as soon as the elves were done with construction. Mephita was pleased to hear this. "Caudata will keep her brother in line, sure enough she will, and straight as a pin she'll keep the home of yours, yes indeed and for certain."

They'd stayed one night at the castle and, while it was perfectly luxurious and comfortable, Dora was pleased to leave the next morning with only Lowell at her side. He'd given her a box, once more wrapped in heavy cream paper and tied with a glossy deep green ribbon. "For you, if it's something you'd like. The elves made it for you at my request."

She'd been surprised and touched to find a garment of the same pattern as his ever-present kilt. "It's an Italian tartan, you see," he'd explained. "As a Rossi, I started wearing a kilt made of it, and I thought, well, since you and I are engaged now…" She'd lifted it and found a buttery-soft wrap dress—angora, he'd informed her—that hugged her curves and fell to her knees in a graceful skirt. "You don't have to wear it," he'd told her. "Not if you don't like it."

"But I love it," she'd insisted, "especially since I'm part of your clan now, Lowell. I want to look like we belong together." She'd kissed him then and thought of the Mathesons in their matching tracksuits and fanny packs, giving each other Eskimo kisses and radiating perfect devotion. *Love is so beautiful when the pieces fall together.*

He promised to take her on a walkabout of the woods and introduce her to trolls, elves, naiads and the other magical beings. "But I'll do it slow and easy," he'd smiled. "No rush, my queen. I want you to drink it all in, in your own sweet time."

A human visitor to the dryad grove, if he or she were to make it this deep into the woods without being frightened away by a glamoured image of a bear, lion or bobcat, would see a patch of a six lush trees in a cluster. That human might notice that the trees bent and swayed without the benefit of a breeze, and he or she might wonder how it was that no dead branches littered the perfect mossy carpet beneath the trunks.

Dora, however, was now one of the Fair Folk and the mysteries of the woods were no longer hidden from her. She saw the trees, but she also saw the dryads who were linked to them. Geneva, the juniper dryad, rested on the moss floor and played a lap harp. Next to her, Hazel, her feet propped on the trunk of her hazel tree, juggled four walnuts. Fiona was in the crook of her tree inspecting the young apples that were swelling on its branches.

"Where are the others?" Dora asked Fiona. She'd been surprised when Fiona had explained earlier that the dryads could safely leave their trees for days at a time to venture into different parts of Prescott Woods.

"Daphne and Dara went to visit the naiads," replied Fiona as she clambered up higher in the tree. "And Ashby's off picking some blackberries for you."

Three walnuts careened over Hazel's head, plopping to the moss beneath her, and one fell on her forehead with a plunk. "That was supposed to be a surprise, Fiona!" Hazel complained, rubbing her head and scowling.

"Oh—whoops! Just pretend you're surprised, okay, Dora?" Fiona's eyes lit up as she parted a group of apple leaves. "This is going to be the best apple crop ever, ladies!"

Geneva strummed a close to her song. "Want back up, Dora? Lowell's still in bed." When Dora nodded, the amenable dryad tilted her head towards her juniper tree and closed her eyes. Immediately, the branches shifted into place so that Dora could ascend with ease.

"Thanks, Geneva." Dora climbed back up and snuggled next to Lowell on the sweet-smelling bed.

The juniper's branches themselves formed the frame and a thick elf-woven pad of rushes served as the padding. The elves were not only talented home-builders and mattress-makers. Lowell had revealed one of their finest inventions — an indiscernible birth control device he wore when they made love. "Just so you don't need to worry," he'd explained gruffly.

From the castle, Lowell had brought along a pillow for each of them and a plush quilt, and Dora had decided on the first night that there was no more desirable bed in the whole world.

"Although," she whispered into Lowell's ear, "the company may have something to do with that." Lowell, eyes shut, grinned and kissed her. "What'll we do today, Lowell? I'm curious about the naiads, and I haven't seen any trolls yet, either. And I'm curious about that leprechaun you were talking about earlier — can we visit him? And what's an Irish sprite doing in Prescott Woods?"

"Sounds like we're going leprechaun hunting," Lowell chuckled. "Even if we don't find the little guy, we can have fun trying. He's more slippery than a gnome. But I've got an idea about what I want to do first." He reached beneath the quilt and cupped one hand around Dora's rear.

"Ahh, so romantic!" a female voice cooed close to Dora's head. She turned to see Geneva in the crook of the tree, smiling blissfully.

"Mm-hm, sure is." Fiona paused in her perusal of the young apples to look over at the juniper tree.

Hazel scampered up the trunk and popped her head over the edge of the mattress. "You guys want any help up here?" She ran her deep green eyes down Lowell's frame and stopped just below his waist. "We know just how Lowell likes it."

"Ah, ladies, many thanks, but not today," Lowell answered. Dora chuckled to see the deep crimson of his cheeks and gave him a fond peck on the cheek. He produced another elven invention from beneath his pillow, commissioned especially for this trip. "We'll see you in a bit, girls." He held aloft a palm-sized green sphere and squeezed its sides. At once, a shimmering tented dome opened over the mattress.

"Aw, phooey," Dora heard Hazel complain from outside the barrier. "They're still shutting us out."

"No matter, Hazel. Come on up into my apple tree and let me see if I can tempt you with something else," Fiona told her. Dora heard the thump-thump of dropping feet and the rustle of leaves in the tree nearest her. "You too, Geneva. Let's play Dora and Lowell, shall we girls? I'll be Dora! Oooh, check out my glossy black hair — I'm sooo beautiful and voluptuous, aren't you jealous?"

"And I'm Lowell!" Hazel chortled in a deep voice. "Arrrgh, arrrgh, arrrgh, lookit my beard! Kinya guess what I've got under this here kilt?"

Geneva giggled with delight. "And I'm me, after Dora and Lowell decide that they'll let us in on their play! Lucky, lucky me — here I come, gonna shake up your tree and strip off your bark! Grr-ruff-ruff-ruff!"

"Dryads." Lowell rolled his eyes and turned to Dora. "They get a little silly here in the woods, I'm afraid."

"Oh, don't be afraid." Dora pulled the quilt off him. "I'm certainly not. They're fun, and who knows what we'll do in the future with them, right Lowell? Forever's a long time." She stroked his thickening erection and lifted her shoulder. "We'll have plenty of chances to try things out in these woods of ours." Lowell's eyes glittered as she straddled him and held his cock between her legs.

"I wish you could see yourself right now, woman. With that shiny deep green behind you, all aglow in the morning light, and your hair falling around your shoulders, and those glorious curves of yours..." He wrapped his hands around her waist and groaned as she eased down onto his shaft. "You're a goddess, Dora. My queen." He ran his hands over her hips and grinned. "Know what you make me think of, lovely lady?" Dora lifted an eyebrow in response. "Whittling."

"Whittling!" she shot back. "The hell you say! I thought you loved my curves, Lowell! And, from what I understand, this figure is as good as it's gonna get, now that I'm one of the Fair Folk. Like it or lump it, Lowell Rossi." She lifted up from his lap until he was barely inside her and glowered at him.

"Oh, hush, Dora! You know good and well that your body excites me like no other woman's possibly could. I love you and I adore the meat on your bones." He squeezed her hips and brought her down a notch or two. "It's just that I realised that being with you makes the world around me make sense. You bring out the best parts of me and let me see the good in everything else. The only other thing that's done that for me is scraping a knife on a piece of oak. I whittled when my father brought me to these woods, transforming our family in one swift stroke, and it helped feel as though I had a little bit of control left in my own life. I thought that if I could make something beautiful out of a chunk of wood, there was something special and worthy about me." He pulled her a bit lower onto his lap. "You make me feel that way, Dora. You're my whittling stick."

"You have a poet's soul, my love, whether you know it or not." She smiled and spread her palms over his broad chest. "And you set me on fire, Lowell. Whittle away—I love being your stick." She lowered herself until he was fully sheathed inside her, then slowly ground her hips against him. Her breasts swayed with the movement and Lowell raised his hands to caress them, then stroked the twisted burn scars on her back.

"I thank all that is good that you are here, well and whole, in my arms," he murmured. Birdsong without the tent mingled with the dryads' giggles of delight.

She smiled and rolled her hips in a tight circle, undulating her stomach as she did when belly dancing with Carmen. Lowell growled and she felt his cock thicken inside her. "Let's take it slow this morning, okay?" she murmured.

Dora clenched her muscles around him and lowered her face to his for a lingering kiss. Lowell flipped her onto her back and traced a path down her neck with the tip of his tongue, then began a slow rhythm that set the tree mattress swinging in the juniper branches.

"That sounds perfect, Dora. We've got all the time in the world."

About the Author

I live in a teeny-tiny town in the southeastern United States, surrounded by rolling hills and lots of cows. My house is brimming with my rowdy sons, hot husband, and more pets than I can shake a stick at. When I close my eyes, though, I'm in a white stucco villa on the Mediterranean, sipping a Pimm's Royal and watching the turquoise waves crash at my feet. Next to my hot husband, naturally.

I love to read and write erotic romance, fantasy, and sci-fi because of the escape factor: I want to leave the ordinary and travel somewhere exotic, unusual, and sexually-charged in a book. My characters are thrust into unpredictable situations, and they respond with humor, open-mindedness, and loads of scorching passion. I hope you enjoy escaping with me into the sultry world of erotic romance.

Bebe Balocca loves to hear from readers. You can find her contact information, website details and author profile page at http://www.totallybound.com.

Totally Bound Publishing